19.95

DISCARD

damage noted

~~stains on b~~

date 9/1/17 init

AROUND THE RUG

AROUND THE RUGGED ROCK

Elizabeth Cadell

Thorndike Press
Thorndike, Maine USA

This Large Print edition is published by Chivers Press, England, and by Thorndike Press, USA.

Published in 1995 in the U.K. by arrangement with the author's estate.

Published in 1995 in the U.S. by arrangement with Brandt & Brandt Literary Agents, Inc.

U.K. Hardcover ISBN 0–7451–3060–7 (Chivers Large Print)
U.K. Softcover ISBN 0–7451–3072–0 (Camden Large Print)
U.S. Softcover ISBN 0–7862–0290–4 (General Series Edition)

The text of this Large Print edition is unabridged.
Other aspects of the book may vary from the original edition.

Set in 16 pt. New Times Roman.

Printed in Great Britain on acid-free paper.

To My Nieces
Jean Verdi, of Paramus, N.J.
and
Alison Petersen, of Cleveland, Ohio

British Library Cataloguing in Publication Data available

Library of Congress Cataloging-in-Publication Data

Cadell, Elizabeth.
  Around the rugged rock / Elizabeth Cadell.
  p. cm.
  ISBN 0–7862–0290–4 (lg. print : lsc)
  1. Large type books. I. Title.
[PR6005.A225A85 1995]
823′.914—dc20   94–26165

CHAPTER ONE

La casa de nuestra señora del carmen is the most beautiful house in all Andalusia.

It was built by the famous soldier, Luis Salvador, on the very spot on which he stood, victorious, watching the last of the vanquished Moors fleeing across the water to the land from which they had come. He had looked about him, and liked what he saw; he gave up campaigning, settled down, made a home, chose a wife and founded a family. Succeeding generations of Salvadors were born at the Casa de Nuestra Señora del Carmen, lived in it, enlarged it and beautified it for the Salvadors who were to come after them. Visitors had come on horses and in coaches and in carriages; now they come in cars along the main Cádiz-Málaga road, and drive for almost two miles beside the pale pink wall that surrounds the estate, and find themselves at the massive, brass-studded doorway, and wait to be admitted.

The high wall and the heavy door are a plain statement of a desire for privacy, and the statement is underlined by the check experienced by visitors on reaching the entrance to the Casa del Carmen. No car enters the ancient portals until its occupants have been scrutinized by the gate-keeper, who is twelve years old and the keeper of a key almost as big as himself. He may confine himself, like a traffic signal, to the simple directions 'stop' or 'go,' or he may request callers to 'wait' an hour or two while I send my sister Conchita up to the house to ask my father to come down here in order that he may see who you are and go up and tell my uncle, who will call his wife to ask the Señora Salvador if you are to be admitted.

The wait may be long, but to those who are finally admitted, it is well worth while. The doors swing back, the visitor enters and finds himself before a second gateway, this time of wrought iron, beautiful in design, through which he glimpses a cool, green luxuriance that gives promise of refreshment in a thirsty land. He follows the drive, winding, shaded by tall eucalyptus trees, and sees round him purple and crimson flowers blazing in the sunshine, and more trees—orange, lemon, olive, chestnut and cork—shading the house. Through a flowering trail of bougainvillia, he sees the blue of the sea and a glimpse of coastline ending in the outline of the Rock of Gibraltar.

The windows of the house look out on one side to the sea, and on the other to the spreading gardens and beyond them, the distant peaks of the Sierra de Ronda. The building is one-storied; a graceful, pale-pink spread of pergola and vine-shaded verandahs and terraces that drop to the edge of the sapphire sea. There is blue sky above, golden sunshine all round and gracious hospitality within.

For these, and other things, the Casa de Nuestra Señora del Carmen is sought by a great many people, especially those within the triangle of Madrid, Málaga and Cádiz. The British, at Gibraltar, stare across the intervening stretch of sea and dream of the pink house in its green setting and long, above all men, for its delights. Those acquainted with Señora Salvador drive joyfully away from the Rock, through the heat and dust of La Linea and out to the cool peace of the lovely old house.

*　　　*　　　*

On a fresh, soft morning in early April, the women were lying on long, cushioned chairs on the terrace outside the drawing-room. Cool drinks were on a table between them; the breeze sighed, the sea murmured and the women talked.

It was a somewhat one-sided conversation, for only the older woman, whose name was Florence van Leyte, showed any real interest in the topic under discussion. The other listened lazily, and with some amusement, to her friend's voice—the voice of a woman with a grievance.

'I did it for the best,' said Florence, with a

3

mixture of bewilderment and defiance. 'How did I know what would happen?'

The younger woman picked up her drink and tried, not very effectively, to submerge the ice cube in it by pushing it down with a straw.

'I told you,' she said, in a placid tone that robbed the words of their usual sting. 'I warned you. I said to you, "Florence, you'll find that they'll never be able to get rid of her." Don't you remember?'

'No, I don't remember, and it's mean to remind me,' said Florence. 'I meant well.'

'That's exactly what you said last time, when you—'

'Lorna, I'm not listening.'

Lorna laughed, and there was a short silence; they sipped their drinks and presently the grey-haired woman looked across, studying her companion.

Lorna Salvador was well worth study. She was the widow of a Spaniard but the daughter of an Englishman, and a large part of her early life had been spent in England. She was a year or two over forty, but the only marks that time had left on her were in a slight tightening of the skin round the high cheek bones, and in a filling-out from youthful slimness to the softer, more generous curves of maturity. If her charming face and long, lovely body had not been enough to admit her to the ranks of beautiful women, her colouring would have given her a place on its own merits. She had

4

skin of a faintly golden shade; her eyes were a deep blue and her hair brown and as yet unflecked with grey. Her skin was flawless, her lips full, humorous and gentle. She looked a kind woman and a rather lazy one; her voice was low and languid, her movements unhurried, her whole air that of a woman with very little to do and a lot of time in which to enjoy doing it.

Beside her, Mrs. van Leyte looked like a well-dressed mummy. She was a woman with a flat, almost ugly face and a figure which, left to itself, sank into comfortable bulges and billows, but it was encased each morning and evening in a foundation garment of great length and steely strength and thus, remoulded, made a well-proportioned frame for Florence's clothes, which were of severe simplicity and impeccable tailoring. Cobweb nylons, good shoes, hair brushed to a glossy smoothness, a skin frankly, skilfully made up; a pair of small, keen, intelligent brown eyes— these combined to make Florence van Leyte into one of those women groomed to a pitch at which mere features were overlooked. She owed nothing to nature and was proud of the fact.

She was a Canadian and had spent the early years of her life in humble circumstances, but she had been twice married, each time to a successful businessman, and now, at fifty-two, was a widow of comfortable means and a kind and generous heart. Her generosity extended beyond the mere giving of alms; though she answered a good many appeals through the medium of her cheque book, there were cases in which she felt the urge to do something more tangible. Her schemes were well-intentioned but ill-advised; she set them in motion with more energy than wisdom, and the majority developed unpleasant boomerang qualities. One of them had just returned, in the form of a letter warm with insults, and Florence was considering it morosely.

'I showed you that appeal, didn't I?' she resumed after a time. 'The one from that charitable society.'

'Yes,' said Lorna. 'But they didn't expect you to—'

'They said that she was destitute, and they wanted a home for her. They said that she was an Austrian and that she'd suffered an awful lot.'

'Yes, Florence, but that didn't mean necessarily—'

'I took it to mean that she'd been in one of those purges. Who wouldn't? They're always finding pockets of the poor things, living in cellars. I thought she'd be old and tiny and broken and crushed and pitiful.'

'But you could have sent her to one of those homes and—'

'How could I? They said she was a princess. You read it yourself. So naturally, I wrote to the snobbiest friends I had and I said now was their chance to show off, the way they liked doing, and do some good at the same time. I said that if they'd just keep her for a bit and build her up—And so they went to meet her, and they took the big car and the chauffeur, and rugs and hot water bottles and an old bottle of smelling salts that they'd hunted up from somewhere. And there she was, fat and overfed and placid, like a cow, and purring like a cat. And now she won't go. They've had her for two months, and they say she's settled in.'

'But they can always—'

'I don't see why they write as though I'd played some kind of trick on them. Nobody's ever written me an abusive letter like that. Well—not quite so abusive.'

'Didn't they write to the society to check up?'

'Of course they did. They wrote and wrote. But all they got was the same old story: yes, this was the one they'd meant; yes, indeed, she'd been through hell; yes, certainly she was a princess, and yes, naturally she was a pauper. So now they've turned on me. What do they think I can do? Pick the woman up and carry her back to wherever she came from?'

Lorna had no suggestions to offer. Her part—a negative one, but performed with a kindness and patience that brought great comfort to Florence—was solely that of a listener. She heard the hopeful beginnings of

Florence's schemes and their ignoble end. There would be an interval, she knew, and Florence would lick her wounds; then there would be fresh appeals and fresh schemes and a great deal of good planned in the worst possible way. An example of her misplaced kindness was living in the house at that moment, Lorna remembered, and Florence must have remembered it at the same moment, for she spoke in a tone that attempted to cover a good deal of doubt.

'How's the child getting on?' she asked.

Lorna took a moment to consider. The child was twenty-seven. Florence had been entertained by her parents in England with such pleasant, not to say ducal, hospitality, that a recent letter from them asking whether she knew anybody who would give their daughter hospitality for a time in return for some secretarial help found her only too ready with a scheme: Lorna had a heavy correspondence and no secretary; she should be given this chance of getting one whose circumstances placed her above the need of a salary. It would be splendid all round; she had never met the daughter, but the parents had spoken of her as a sweet child; she would be a sweet help and companion to Lorna, and some of the ducal kindness would be repaid. Florence had duly driven out to the airport at Gibraltar and returned with an inscrutable expression and a tall, dark young woman with glasses, a severe look and the manner of an inspector looking into faulty drains. She explained at once that she disliked being called Rose and wished to be known by her second name, which was Stephanie. She took down Lorna's faltering dictation, improved the grammar, polished up the phrasing and produced results remarkable in their pomposity. Lorna signed them without comment and added humanizing postscripts and wished very much that she had been more energetic in opposing the scheme from the start.

Stephanie's conversation—outside her rigorously kept working hours—dealt almost exclusively with her fiancé, who was called Sven Hardensen and who had, for reasons not too clear, gone on a whaling expedition; in his absence she had felt herself called upon to do some useful work, and Lorna, signing the work with a sigh, fell to wondering how much time would elapse before a man could return from a whaling expedition, if he had any intention of returning.

'Stephanie?' she said at last, in answer to Florence's question. 'Oh, she seems to be getting on all right.'

She saw Florence's eyes on her and looked steadily elsewhere. Not yet. Not this morning, when poor Florence was smarting under the insults of those she had called her friends. For this moment, at least, her troubles would come

9

singly.

Florence spoke in the tone of one answering an unspoken accusation.

'She looks pretty efficient—you can't deny that, can you?'

'I didn't deny it,' pointed out Lorna mildly.

'But I suppose,' went on Florence, groping, 'I should have taken a look at her before I asked you to have her.'

'Oh—I don't know.'

'The thing that gets my goat,' said Florence, advancing into the open, 'is the way she talks to me. You'd think she was a health visitor going round the padded cells.'

'I don't think health—'

'That's neither here nor there, Lorna. I don't mind how much she looks down her nose at me, but if I thought she tried to—'

'I don't think you should worry about her. She's simply one of those people who likes to see things done a certain way.'

'Her way. Lorna, d'you suppose that Swede is hiding out somewhere?'

Lorna thought it probable, but she refrained from saying so. Instead, she brought Florence back to a safer topic.

'What are you going to write and say to those people who've written to you?' she asked.

'About that Austrian? Nothing,' said Florence. 'If I write back straight away, I'll say something I'd be sorry for later. That's the way to start a fight. I'll just let them think I didn't get the letter, and that'll do them out of a lot of satisfaction.'

They considered this complicated piece of reasoning for some time, and then Florence spoke again in a voice of unusual humility.

'You know, Lorna,' she said, 'it just struck me that when you look at it, I'm just as bad as that woman. I came here for a short visit, and look at me—I'm still here, and showing no signs of taking off. But there's a difference; at least you know that I've got somewhere else to go to if you ever wanted to drop a hint. I could go back to Canada and give my relations a nice surprise—well, a surprise. Or I could do that trip I was going to do when I dropped in here eight months ago. Eight months—'

'It doesn't feel as long as that,' said Lorna, with perfect honesty. 'I've liked having you here.'

She finished her drink and prodded the various fruits at the bottom of the glass, and a servant came forward from the shadows and was about to pour her out another one when she stopped him.

'No, Carlos,' she said. 'No more.'

She lifted her arms in a long, lazy stretch, and Florence roused herself and spoke hastily.

'You're not going inside yet, are you?'

'Yes, I was.'

'Well, wait a minute. I really came out here to tell you something,' said Florence. 'Only that rude letter put it out of my head.'

11

'What is it?' asked Lorna. 'More bother for you?'

'No. Nothing that concerns me at all— though I should hate to be left out of it altogether. It's about that love-affair that isn't going so well. Your little friend Carmela Fernandez.'

For the first time Lorna sat up and looked across at the other woman with real interest in her glance.

'What about her?' she asked.

'Well, I went into Gib yesterday, and I met that young man she's in love with—that naval officer who's giving her father all that trouble. He was at the party, and half-way through it, someone must have told him that I lived with you, because he'd been looking at me without seeing me, and he suddenly came at me as if I'd been the only woman in the room. He went straight to the point, I'll say that for him. He said he wanted to come out and meet you.'

'What's he like?' asked Lorna.

'He's—you know, I don't wonder Carmela's in love with him, Lorna. He really is a heart breaker. He's tall and tanned and he's got eyes something like yours, only they're even more effective in a man's face.'

'How did you know he was the one Carmela was in love with?'

'I told you, he said it straight out. He said he'd heard that I was a friend of yours and that you were a friend of hers and so he wanted to

12

be a friend of ours. Most young men would have come round to it by way of a compliment or two, but not this man. I wished I'd known more of the affair, so's I could have talked to him about it, but I only knew what you'd told me, and that wasn't much.'

'I told you all I knew. Carmela didn't have much time to explain, poor little thing. All she said was that she'd fallen in love with this young man from Gibraltar—she didn't even tell me his name.'

'Is her father really against it, Lorna?'

'He's not exactly pleased about it. He's got other ideas for Carmela, that's all.'

'I can't for the life of me see why. If this young Englishman is whole in mind and body and estate—especially in estate—why shouldn't Carmela marry him?'

'For lots of reasons. But it's difficult to make them sound sensible to anybody who hasn't lived with Spaniards for as long as I have. The Spanish family isn't a unit, like the English family; it's a spreading affair that takes in uncles and aunts and cousins so far removed that you and I wouldn't consider them as relations at all. I called it spreading, but I only meant in numbers, because in other ways it isn't spreading at all—it's compact. It's so compact that it's difficult for an outsider to break into. There's so much family in Spain that the average Spanish family doesn't as a rule throw its door open to foreigners. They

13

welcome them, they offer hospitality, but they don't expect them to—'

'Count themselves in?'

'No.'

'I counted myself in here, didn't I? But then, you're not Spanish.'

'Half.'

'I never think of you as even half Spanish. But everyone who doesn't know you, thinks you are. I think this young man does. I forgot to tell him you weren't.'

'Does it matter?'

'Yes. He's coming to see you.'

Lorna's eyes opened wide, and she looked across in surprise.

'When?'

'This morning. That's what I came out to tell you, only I never got round to it.'

'This morning! Good gracious! What for? Oh yes, of course ...'

'That's it. He found out—he didn't say how, but I suppose it was through Carmela—that you're an intimate friend of her family, and he's coming to enlist your support.'

Lorna smiled, stretched once more and rose gracefully from her chair. She walked to the balustrade and stood with her back to Florence, looking across to the distant Rock, on which the subject of their conversation was doubtless dreaming of his Carmela.

'I shan't be here when he comes,' said Florence. 'I promised him you'd be alone. I'll

14

drive into Málaga, and I'll take Stephanie with me and give her lunch there—if she'll do me the honour. Do you want me to buy anything for you while I'm there?'

Lorna considered.

'No,' she said at last. 'Nothing that I can think of at the moment.'

'Then I'll get going.' Florence rose. 'Be nice to him, Lorna, and ask him to come again. He's the most handsome young man I ever saw.'

'That's what Carmela said, only not quite in those words.'

'Well, she's right. They'd make a wonderful pair, Lorna, and you really ought to go in strongly on their side. You can do anything with Don Manrique and his wife.'

'Not anything.'

'Yes, you can. You can make them see reason, and you can persuade them to let their daughter get married without all this fuss. If I knew any Spanish—oh, her father speaks English, doesn't he?'

'Yes.'

'Well, next time I see him coming in to see you, I'll put in a word for the lovers. Now Lorna, remember what I said. Don't rush this business. Spin it out so's we can all get a good look at the young man. 'Bye for now.'

'Oh—Florence!' Lorna turned and called, and Florence, on her way into the house, paused and glanced over her shoulder.

15

'Well?'

'You didn't tell me his name,' said Lorna.

'Nicholas.'

'Yes,' said Lorna, 'but there must be some more.'

'Nicholas Saracen,' said Florence, and went into the house.

And Lorna Salvador, on the terrace, stared after her with the blood draining slowly from her face and her eyes wide and fixed with something not far from panic.

Nicholas. Nicholas Saracen. He was coming here. He was coming ... soon ... now. She would be face to face with him; she would see him, hear him, be near enough to touch him. She felt herself trembling at the thought and made a desperate attempt to regain her self-command. She forced herself to look forward and saw their meeting as it would be—a young man coming to meet an unknown woman, a young man anxious to talk about himself and his love. Nicholas—in love. Nicholas, Nicholas, Nicholas—

The moments passed, but Lorna stood still, quieter now, and with a new feeling welling up from the bottom of her heart. Nicholas—she was to see him. That was all that she need think about at present. A smile curved her lips; it was tremulous at first, but it grew wider; a light of expectancy came into her eyes and the colour came back to her cheeks. She found herself free from apprehension and lifted up with pure happiness. Nicholas...

Joyously, she went inside to prepare for his arrival.

CHAPTER TWO

Nicholas allowed himself plenty of time. With his car, one never knew; she might make it, or she might not. The engine didn't sound in too good a mood, so he'd better allow for accidents. It wouldn't do to be late. This Señora Salvador was already somebody fairly important in her own right; as a friend of Carmela, she took on even more weight; as a possible mediator between himself and the flinty, callous individual who was privileged to be Carmela's father, she acquired a value almost impossible to estimate.

He changed out of his uniform and chose the grey flannel trousers with the sharpest crease. His sports coat was just back from the cleaner's—but this was no casual, jacket-and-flannels lunch. This edged over into one of these morning-suit affairs; he was to look smart, not to say slick, the kind of man Señora Salvador would be proud to sponsor. A suit was the thing.

Since he only had two suits, Nicholas was not long in choosing; he put on the grey. His shirt was snowy, his navy tie neat, his shoes

17

burnished beyond reproach. His hair ... it stood up a bit, but that might be nervousness. He gave himself a final look-over and felt reasonably satisfied. Nobody could say that he didn't look like a scion—what *was* a scion, incidentally?—of one of England's best, or well, let's face it, as Señora Salvador might want to know, one of England's second-best families. Handkerchief ... a last going-over with a clothes brush, and—yes, that was the lot.

He drove fast and bore with less patience than usual the hold-ups at the successive frontier barriers. He drew up at the Spanish customs and waited behind a car laden with purchases from Gibraltar. The routine was familiar, but it still amused Nicholas.

'Anything?' enquired the official, staring in at openly displayed goods.

The driver produced a note, and it changed hands.

'Nothing.'

The car moved on, and Nicholas drove up into its place. A corrupt system, if you looked at it one way, he mused. But that wasn't the way they looked at it; it was merely part of the day's work—and the day's pay.

'Anything?'

'Nothing.' Not even a tip, my poor fellow.

He was through. A further hold-up at the Cádiz-Málaga cross-roads and he was clear, and speeding in the direction of the Casa de

18

Nuestra Señora del Carmen.

He wondered, as he drove, what Señora Salvador would be like. He had been in Gibraltar for a month, but for three weeks of that time he had been in love, and so out of touch with social life. He knew that the Casa del Carmen was spoken of as a house of unparalleled distinction and charm, and he had gathered that its owner lent it an added grace. The Governor of Gibraltar visited it frequently, and he had also heard the admiral speak of dinner-parties there and had noted, with some surprise, his tone of wistful reminiscence. This visit, he felt, was going to be interesting, but was it, he wondered with a sudden pang, was it going to be productive? He was trying to be patient, as Carmela had begged him to, but he was making little progress with his courtship, and he was not going to be at Gibraltar indefinitely. Another month—another five weeks for the refit and the *Panther* would be ready. Another six weeks and he would be sweating in eastern waters, far away from Carmela. Things had got to move and to move fast.

He reached the bend in the road that led down to the little fishing village of Estronella and brought the car to a stop. This was almost it. It was certainly a view—the single village street, the white row of fishermen's cottages, the boats drawn up out of the water; to the left, the beginning of the pale pink wall of the Casa

19

del Carmen; beyond, the sea, with a clear view across to the Rock, which—from here—looked a good deal less rugged and imposing.

Nicholas stayed there, looking a little, thinking a lot, and then gave a sigh. He must get on. The Canadian woman—what was her name?—van Leyte—had said that there would be no difficulty about admittance. In cases of this sort, she had said, the doors opened at a touch.

Nicholas found that this statement was correct. His summons brought an instant and gratifying response. The grille on the huge door was drawn cautiously aside; a small nose appeared and seemed to sniff. White teeth flashed a welcome, and then, with a high squeaking and a low grinding, the great door opened, and a small boy and two smaller girls appeared and waved Nicholas through with ceremonious dignity. He produced his single word of Spanish, spoken with the Castilian lisp and giving the impression that there were plenty more where that came from.

'Gracias!'

If only it weren't so convincing! If only it didn't always inaugurate a stream of happy chat and an endless succession of unintelligible phrases. But one could always smile and look knowing. Looking as knowing as possible, Nicholas drove through the second gate, followed the curves of the drive and drew up at the wide flight of steps that led up to the main

20

hall of the house.

Servants, he noted, sprang out from nowhere in the well-established rub-of-the-lamp tradition. He had an odd feeling of being passed from hand to hand, endlessly, and then he found himself at the door of a room and knew, by the increase of dignity on the part of his escorts, that his hostess was within.

He drew a deep breath and squared his shoulders. Ceremony was all very well, but he mustn't let it impress him too much. She might be a queen in her own domain, but for the moment she was merely Carmela's friend and all he wanted—he must make it clear from the beginning—all he wanted was a spoke put in the wheel of that antiquated, feudal, obstructive, superfluous Don Manrique Fernandez, who could see nothing attractive in the idea of his daughter's marrying into Her Majesty's Navy.

The door before him opened, and the servants stood aside. Nicholas entered and went forward into what he took, at first, to be a vast but empty room. Then, at the far end of it, standing against a long window, he saw his hostess and walked forward to meet her.

Lorna waited, watching him as he came. He looked older than she had expected and—in spite of his considerable height and adequate width—smaller, for she had looked for something of his father's massiveness, and it was not there. This man—for he was a man,

21

and not the boy she had almost hoped to see—was large, but he was lean; his shoulders were broad, but they were not of the ox-like width and strength of his father's. There was strength here, but not that instant suggestion of power. Lorna, who had filled the doorway with a picture of his father, found the frame too wide and stood silently making adjustments.

As he came nearer she saw and recognized the colour and set of the eyes, the sweep of jaw, the mobile, humourous mouth. His expression, too, she had seen before, and she found she could still interpret it: he was unsure of his reception but certain of his ability to charm her; he had put on his cloak of diffidence and good manners, and from behind it he was peering at her, weighing her up, deciding how much of his force he would need and how best he could apply it. As their eyes met, dark blue to darker blue, she found herself swept back, back—and once more she was controlling her desire to laugh with him, and resisting it and fitting on, instead, her air of common sense, of judicial impartiality. Something unexpected—a surge of delight—shook her for an instant, and then she heard his voice.

'It's—it's most awfully good of you to let me come.'

A nice touch: warm, impetuosity held in check. Nobody could have done it better. How could that great, raw, boorish, direct-approach-only father produce a son with a

22

whole armoury of charm? There was an answer, and Lorna had no hesitation in supplying it. Charm? But naturally . . .

She held out her hand, and he took it. The slight bow was his way of showing her that he knew what was due to foreigners: an added touch of grace and deference.

'How do you do?' she said. 'Will you sit down? I think you'd like that chair best.'

She was pleased to see him thrown, for a moment, completely off his balance. His stare was almost a gape.

'Why, you're—Good Lord, you're English!' he said.

She smiled and settled herself with her slow, easy grace into a low chair. Against its soft colours, her white dress and golden skin showed up with a perfection he noted and appreciated.

'Yes,' she answered him. 'Didn't you know?'

'Well, no. I—'

'Mrs. van Leyte should have told you.'

'I suppose she thought I knew. It did strike me—once—that the name she called you— Lorna—wasn't particularly Spanish, but I didn't realize—'

'Of course you wouldn't,' she said gently. 'You had your own affairs to think about.'

He eyed her for a moment and saw nothing in her glance but kindly interest.

'I—yes. I do hope you'll forgive me for bothering you with them, but—' He hesitated, and then decided to plunge directly to the heart of the matter. 'As a matter of fact, I've come to a dead end. I'm stuck. I can't get any further, and I'm certainly not going to go back.'

'You seem to have come quite a long way in a short time,' commented Lorna, with a touch of dryness. 'It isn't easy for a stranger, a foreigner, to get into the family circle of Spaniards. It's a—'

'Closed corporation. Yes, I fully understood that from the start. But I had a—well, a kind of initial advantage, you know.'

'What kind?' she enquired.

'The most wonderfully lucky—the most amazing, the most romantic kind.' He leaned forward, his face alight with eagerness. 'Can I tell you?'

'I'm waiting.'

'She was riding. She was—Well, girls in England look—you know how girls go out hacking, looking pretty good in neat riding kit? Well, she didn't look like that at all. She looked—She wasn't alone. She had a sort of groom trotting along behind, and they were coming down the hillside, down one of those mule tracks. I was in my car on the main road, and I just happened to glance up, and when I saw her, I jammed on the brakes and just sat there, looking. She had on one of those hats— you know?'

'I know.'

'Sort of South American, with strings

coming down under her chin, and a—a coloured scarf round her neck, and one of those skirts and boots and—'

Recollection, flooding in, choked him. He gazed abstractedly down at his own footwear, and Lorna, her eyes roaming over him, was content to wait.

'I sat there,' he went on presently, 'and she looked up ... down ... and saw me. I didn't dare move, I thought that if I made a movement of any sort, she'd think I was making passes—waving—and so I kept quite still, and after a little while, she—smiled at me. Then they went on, they crossed the track and began to canter, and I thought I'd better get along, and so I started up the car and—'

'Ah,' said Lorna. 'I think I heard it this morning, when you arrived.'

'Yes. It always sounds pretty awful, but when it starts up, it's worse than the wrath of God. I must have been mad to have forgotten that the horses were so near, but I wasn't quite in my right mind. And the car came to life, and the next thing I saw was the groom vanishing over the skyline. He could ride; by golly, he could ride, but he was on a mad horse, and all he could do was—'

'Over the skyline.'

'Yes. And she—Her horse had reared, and she looked like one of those pictures—But I saw that if someone didn't do something, however magnificently she was managing the

25

brute, she'd—'

'Over the skyline.'

He checked, and she smiled at him.

'I'm listening,' she said.

'I suppose you think I'm out of my mind?'

'Yes,' she said gently. 'But go on. Or perhaps I can go on. You got out of the car that sounds like a fire engine, and you rushed up the hillside to the rescue of a girl who can probably give points to every other horsewoman in Spain, and you frightened her horse still further by hanging yourself on to its bridle.'

'I suppose so. But she dismounted, and we stood there, and we waited for the groom to reappear.'

'And he did?'

'No. Only his horse. It looked, as it were, meant, don't you think?'

'Preordained?'

'Definitely. There we were, she and I, riding home together. I left my car on the road, and her father could do no less than send a man down to fetch it.'

'How were you received?'

His eyes clouded, and he looked at her with an appeal that pulled at her heart. She had seen that look before—often; so often, when he had been in mischief, when he was in trouble, when his well-ordered affairs went awry. Before she could stop herself, she had put out a hand to lay it for an instant, lightly, on his cheek. She checked the gesture at its beginning, but, as

26

though he remembered, the movement seemed to give him reassurance, and he went on in a lighter tone.

'That's what I've come to see you about,' he said. 'I'm not.'

'Not received?'

'No. Or only barely. As I said, I've come to a dead end. I'm in love—who wouldn't be, with her? She's—'

'I know all about her,' said Lorna. 'I've known her since she was eight, and I've seen her more or less constantly ever since, so I don't think you need bother about descriptions. If you'll tell me how far you've got—'

'I don't think I ever really got further than I did on that first day,' said Nicholas. 'They had to receive me then—I was a benefactor, in a sense. I'd brought home their daughter. They made it clear, in the most courteous way, that they couldn't see that there'd been any need for my services, but they were kind enough to thank me and to offer me some wine and to have my car fetched for me. But there was none of that do-come-again, or pop-in-any-time-you're-passing. They were polite, they were kind, they even pretended they were grateful, but when I drove up a day or so later with a sheaf of lilies, looking like an Easter bride, there was a change. There was a distinct cooling down on the part of Don Manrique. The temperature had dropped, and it's been

27

dropping ever since.'

'Perhaps'—Lorna's eyes mocked him—
'they didn't like you?'

'Nonsense,' said Nicholas.

'I suppose you know,' she said, 'that you're
up against something quite difficult?'

'Certainly I do. This happened three weeks
ago, and I've had to fight like a team of tomcats
every time I've wanted to see her. If she hadn't
felt as I did, if she hadn't done everything she
could to help me—But now she says—'

'I know what she says. You haven't
forgotten, have you, that I'm an intimate
friend of the family? Isn't that why you came to
see me?'

'Can you do anything?' asked Nicholas.

'I don't know. You're up against some really
stubborn parental opposition.'

'On both sides,' said Nicholas gloomily.

'I thought that Carmela's mother was with
you and not against you.'

'I didn't mean her mother or her father.'

She stared at him for some moments without
speaking, and then put a question.

'Then what do you mean by both sides?'

'I meant my own family.'

Lorna drew a quick breath.

'But—'

'I've got a father,' said Nicholas, without
enthusiasm. 'In England. He doesn't know the
first thing about Carmela, but he's dead
against it.'

'And why?'

'Well—you see, he got wind of it from some half-baked admiral he met in his club in London. The admiral had been at Gib and took home all the details, and my father thinks I've fallen into a gang of cut-throats—or worse.'

'Gang of—?' She gave a little shrug. 'I don't understand.'

He looked slightly uncomfortable, and then spoke with his eyes on hers.

'It's this smuggling business,' he said. 'I don't like to suggest that there's anything in it, but it's very strongly rumoured in Gibraltar that Carmela's father is the boy at the head of the biggest and best of the local smuggling rackets.'

'Carmela's father?'

'Yes.'

'Don Manrique?'

'Yes. I know he's a friend of yours, and I don't want to suggest for a moment that he's a—'

'But of *course* he is!' said Lorna. 'Do you mean you didn't know?'

'I—' Nicholas looked across at her and laughed. 'I felt pretty sure he was, but I didn't know how you—'

'It's a time-honoured profession,' said Lorna.

'In these parts, yes. But try to imagine what it would sound like to my father, just coming

29

out from behind his paper at the club. His son chasing a smuggler's daughter. I can see his mind working.'

'So can I.'

'He'd start off on rum-running and reject that. He'd go on to drugs and hang there like a leech. His letters don't say so, but they breathe opium and heroin and marijuana. A nice situation, don't you think? Her father here, determined to marry her off to a nice young, rich, suitable, Spanish fellow. My father over there, hinting strongly at pulling strings to have me moved from Gib and put on a slow boat to China. He can do it, too. He's got a lot of those Admiralty boys in his pocket. So you see, I'm between the devil and the deep blue sea. I'm stuck with two fathers, and I can't do anything, but you can get through the only chink in the armour-plated entrance. That is, if you will.'

'You mean Carmela's mother, I suppose?'

'Yes. Carmela loves me, and both her parents know it, but only her mother believes it. I don't know how much influence her mother has over her papa, but you'd know. I know it's the most appalling impertinence to ask you, and I shall understand if you refuse to do anything, but Carmela had always spoken of you as an old and trusted friend of theirs, and when I found that Mrs. van Leyte lived here with you, I—Can you do anything?'

'I could try.'

'I don't know why you should. You don't know much about me.'

'Not much,' admitted Lorna. 'But—something. I—knew you when you were a little boy.'

'Good Lord! You did? How small?' demanded Nicholas.

'Oh, four, five. You and your brother Martin.'

Her eyes left his and lifted to the view beyond him, but he saw that she was not thinking of the view. After a moment she rose and walked to a small table and picked up a box of cigarettes and held them out to him with a little air of apology.

'I'm sorry about these,' she said. 'I don't smoke, and so I forget about other people. The lighter's over there.'

Nicholas took the box from her and put it back on the table.

'Never mind about cigarettes,' he said, slowly. 'You said you knew me when I was four or five?'

'Yes.'

'In that case, would you very much mind telling me something?'

'If I can,' said Lorna.

'It may sound an odd question, but did you know my mother?'

She had walked slowly out of the room and on to the terrace, and he followed her, and she turned to answer him. She was leaning against

31

the balustrade, and her pose was easy, casual and unconsciously graceful. His eyes went over the lovely figure and came to rest on her face.

'Yes,' she said at last. 'I knew your mother. Do you remember her?'

'No. You see, she—when I was very young, she left my father.'

'Why?' she asked coolly.

'I don't—they didn't get on,' said Nicholas. 'But he never spoke of her, and there weren't any photographs, and nobody I met ever seemed to have known anything about her. You're the first—'

There was a pause.

'You weren't a nice little boy,' said Lorna dreamily. 'You used to tell the most man-sized lies without a blush. You were big for your age and tough, and even at that age you knew what charm could do—and you used to use yours quite deliberately, as you do now. You were cock-sure and self-sufficient, and the only time you needed anybody was when you got into trouble—and then you chose the person who could be the most use to you, and you went to them and made them help you, as you still do. Nobody could do much for you when things were going well. No, you were on your feet, well and firmly on your feet. But Martin—' A smile curved her lips. 'Martin was different. He didn't have confident blue eyes; he had big, sad, haunting grey ones, with inch-long lashes. He had fat little fists that clutched at you. He always shared everything—his hopes, his troubles, anything he had in the way of ideas. He was small and soft and infinitely embraceable. He had no life of his own—not then. He always liked something solid for his little fists to grasp. That's the kind of little boy that pulls the heart out of you, not your sort of little boy.'

He was staring at her, and he had taken a step and then remained still, and she went on speaking calmly.

'It was obvious,' she said, 'that you'd always be able to look out for yourself. Quite obvious. Nauseatingly obvious. But nobody could hold Martin in their arms without feeling his dependence—and dependence, may I point out, is a very much more lovable quality than pushiness. Dear Martin.'

'Oh, God,' said Nicholas, very softly.

'I never had much feeling about seeing you again, but I used to wake up and imagine Martin looking, feeling, calling.'

His arms were on her shoulders, and he had forced her to look at him. Her gaze was calm and her voice quiet.

'He couldn't talk properly,' she said. 'He was getting along, but he was only two—going on for three—and things like hospital and bicycle and signal used to trip him up. And hellifump. He was convinced that a hellifump had two tails. How long was it before he learned that they hadn't, poor Martin?'

33

'Look at me,' said Nicholas gently.

'I'm looking. But you haven't changed, you know. You're still disgustingly master of yourself and your life, and when anything goes wrong, when anything falls out of place, you pick up somebody and use them for a time, don't you?'

'Yes,' said Nicholas. His hands slid down and encircled her and drew her close.

'My eyes,' said Lorna, looking into his.

'Yes.'

'And my mouth.'

'Yes.'

'And my charm. Your father never had any.'

'You're beautiful,' said Nicholas. 'I always hoped you would be. But as I got older, I began to feel that I'd be too late to see you as I wanted to see you. I counted up how old you'd be.'

'I look thirty,' said Lorna, her finger tracing the lines of his face. 'I thought you'd be broader, like your father, but I'm glad you're not.'

'Do I look anything like you?'

'Yes. Where's Martin?'

'Never mind Martin. I'm here. I feel—'

'Well?'

'I can't explain. Just—Thank god,' said Nicholas.

'Yes. But there's something else I'd like you to say. And you might kiss me. I don't know how it was, but you always used to be sticky, even directly after your bath. Say it, please,

34

Nicholas.'

'Darling Mother,' said Nicholas, and bent and kissed her gently.

CHAPTER THREE

'He was a brute,' said Lorna, over lunch. 'From the beginning to the end, a brute. He snatched me from the cradle, married me before I was old enough to know what was happening to me, and presented me with two babies before I was twenty. He—'

'Didn't *you* present *him*?' enquired Nicholas.

'If you're going to interrupt me in the middle of a harrowing story just to argue about points of grammar,' she said, 'then I shan't go on, and you'll be left to grope for the rest of your life in the half-truths and the misrepresentations they've fed you with all these years. I thought that while we were alone, I could tell you the real truth.'

'Alone?' said Nicholas.

His mother, he knew, felt them to be alone. They were lunching together in a shady part of the terrace; Carlos and Natalio were serving them, and Lourdes and Joselita busied themselves at a side table on which were a variety of dishes and a towering basket of fruit.

'Well, almost alone,' amended Lorna.

They looked at one another and laughed,

and she saw in her son's eyes a clear indication that she was all he had hoped his mother would be—and more. Nicholas was, indeed, content; he had come to visit a stranger and engage her assistance in the acquisition of a wife; instead, he had found a mother and he was looking, for the moment, not forward but back into the extremely interesting past. He had put Carmela, just for a time, at the back of his mind while he got to know this woman facing him across the table, her lovely face framed in a shady hat, her eyes smiling into his as she made it clear that the breaking-up of their life as a family was in no way her fault. She was—he had to understand—the innocent victim; she had done nothing, and his father was responsible for everything.

'He was old enough to be my father,' went on Lorna. 'I was a girl of seventeen and he was an enormous, unfeeling man of well over thirty and—'

'Thirty-two,' slipped in Nicholas neatly.

'I weighed not quite a hundred pounds, and he was about twice that. More. Can you imagine? He was so wide, that if I stood behind him I was completely hidden. He—he *towered*. And he took me, young, inexperienced and defenceless, from a happy—from several happy homes and put me into a mouldering mansion and—'

'Wychall House?' asked Nicholas, in genuine surprise.

'Wychall House.' Lorna shuddered. 'Did you go on living there?'

'No. At least, not for a time.'

'I'm so glad. It wasn't a house to bring children up in. And your father's two dreadful sisters weren't fit to have the care of young children.'

'*Dreadful*? Aunt Heloise and Aunt Kate?'

'Quite, quite dreadful—Nicholas, take some more chicken, please—yes, dreadful, because they ruined my life.'

Nicholas glanced round him. The sea shimmered and danced; the great, pale pink house stood among its trees and flowers. The sun shone.

'This, at any rate,' he said, his glance gently mocking, 'isn't a mouldering mansion.'

'This is the—the other side of the river, as it were,' said Lorna. 'But the river itself, if I may be poetical, was most unpleasant, and it was your father and his two horrid sisters who—who pushed me into it.'

'That isn't really poetry, Mother darling.'

' "Mother darling ... Mother darling," ' murmured Lorna happily. She gave him a smile of such love and delight that Nicholas felt his heart give a twist. 'You know, Nicholas, it's almost worth it—it almost makes up for everything to have a large, not-far-from-handsome son with me now, listening to me and calling me "Mother darling." But you know, it can't wipe out the fact that your father

37

behaved like a—like a monster. He accused me of—of unspeakable things. He judged me without a hearing. He listened to the spiteful, narrow gossip of two sour old women and—'

'They weren't quite forty,' murmured Nicholas, into his wineglass.

'Well, perhaps they weren't,' admitted Lorna reluctantly, 'but they seemed old to me when I was seventeen. And they hated me. In my cooler moment, when it was all over, I saw why. I was a foreigner—not in nationality, because although I had a Spanish mother, my father was English. But he died when I was fifteen, and as soon as he was buried, my mother, who loathed English life and only bore it because she loved my father, went back to Spain. It wasn't new to me—I'd visited my mother's relations several times—but it was different to go back and to settle down into a family life with all my Spanish connections. I was very happy; my father had no relations to speak of, so there was nothing to draw us back to England. I thought I was in Spain for ever, and I was very glad. I loved Madrid, and I loved several of my handsome young cousins. I was just beginning to look beyond cousins when your father—of all unlikely people— came to Madrid on business. He couldn't speak a word of Spanish, but, being your father, he was convinced that even without a word of the language he'd make a better job of it than someone who was fluent. One of my

uncles asked him out to lunch in the country—
and I was there. He never took his eyes off me,
and I found myself staring at him. I thought he
was a showpiece. He had fists like those hams
you hang up, and shoulders … We were
lunching out of doors, as you and I are now,
and his back was to the house, and he blotted
out eight windows and my aunt's
summerhouse. It was fantastic. My mother
was in Madrid, and I was in charge of my uncle
and aunt, who didn't speak a word of English,
but your father had a dictionary, and he looked
up the words for niece and love and marriage
and caused a terrible commotion, but it was no
use all my uncles and cousins trying to talk him
down, because he didn't understand a word of
what they said. He got me alone in my mother's
house and proposed to me and we were
married. I was seventeen and he was—'

' "An enormous, unfeeling man of well over
thirty." '

'Yes. We came to England and I expected,
naturally, that I'd live the pleasant sort of life
I'd led with my father when he was alive. But I
was taken to Wychall and installed as a merely
nominal mistress in that great, ugly, depressing
house, with Heloise and Kate, who'd been
born in it and thought it was beautiful. The
cook was sixty, the housemaids were eighty
and the gardener could scarcely walk. There
was no music and no gaiety of any sort—in
fact, there was no noise at all. It was all quiet

dignity and rusty black. It was death. Your father was never there because his work was abroad, and I was lonely and miserable. And I was seventeen. I suppose they told you that I couldn't fit in and that I chose to go away?'

'Nobody,' said Nicholas, 'ever told me anything. Go on.'

'I had two babies. The first one wasn't a great success, but the next one showed a great improvement. And I enjoyed having them. They gave me something to do and something to love. The nurseries were in the nicest, the lightest part of the house, and I had a young nurse and a young nursemaid and—in that part of the house—you could actually hear laughter and occasionally song. Babies were fun and a good excuse for getting out of the terrible county goings-on. It wasn't exciting for a young girl, but I was happy. And then one of my cousins came to England on a visit and brought a friend. My cousin went back to Spain, but his friend—a charming, handsome young Spaniard—stayed on in England, working in a firm in London, and because I was a link with everything he knew and loved in Spain, he used to come down almost every week-end and stay at Wychall. Your father was abroad; your two aunts didn't like him and said so plainly and so unpleasantly that I didn't tell them that he—Juan—was engaged to marry a friend of mine in Madrid and was longing to get back to her. He talked to me of nothing else. But he came too often, and we laughed too much, and nobody could understand what we said, because his English was so bad that it was more sensible to talk Spanish, and at last your aunts wrote to your father and told him that they feared the worst. You know, Nicholas, I didn't dream that talking about it now, after all these years, could make me so angry.'

'Never mind, you look nice when you're angry. Go on.'

'I'm going on. You're going to hear the truth, and then you'll realize what a monster you have for a father. They've let you imagine the worst about me; now you can learn who was responsible for it all.'

'My father.'

'Yes. He swallowed his sisters' suspicions without so much as a thought of disapproving them. He was in Africa, on business that he thought was too important to leave in order to clear his wife's name. He wrote to me—a letter that killed every spark of affection I ever had for him. He held forth on the additional responsibilities of a wife whose husband was away from home. He talked meaningless rubbish about extreme youth and hot Latin blood, and he ended by saying that he was not a man who would tolerate unfaithfulness in a wife.'

'He was merely, I suppose, trying to—'

'He used the word. Unfaithfulness. His letter

41

said, as clearly as though he'd written the words down, that he believed the worst. He could take a seventeen-year-old girl away from a happy environment, bury her in a remote country house of the most archaic and uncomfortable type; he could leave her with prejudiced and unsympathetic companions, he could make her the mother of his children and leave her alone for months at a time—and then, at the first whisper of malicious gossip, he could go over to the enemy and accuse his wife of unfaithfulness. Is that a husband? Is that a man at all?'

'He lacks finesse,' said Nicholas, 'but if you'd—'

'He took matters out of my hand. He had written an unforgivable letter to me, but that was only one thing. He wrote in the same strain to my mother and to my uncle, and *that* was the end. Because he was so wrapped up in his notions about his own honour that he'd forgotten that the Spanish are a race who have honourable notions of their own—and a fire and a temper quite beyond anything that a mere Englishman can understand. My mother would have been discreet; she would have said nothing and merely come to England to see me, to help me. But the letter to my uncle finished everything, because his daughter was the girl to whom Juan was engaged. And now you can count the lives your father and his wicked sisters destroyed. Mine, of course. But my mother's, too, for she never really got over it. My cousin's, for her father at once broke off her engagement to Juan. Juan's, because he was deeply in love and innocent of everything he'd been accused of. And last of all, Juan's mother. She adored him, but—like your father—she believed the worst, and she never forgave him or me. All that unhappiness, all that waste, all that tragedy, simply because two old women saw everything in a hateful, twisted way and a husband had no faith in his wife.'

There was silence. Nicholas took a cigarette from the box that Carlos was holding out to him and accepted a light from Natalio. Leaning back, he looked across at his mother: She was leaning forward with her elbows in the table, and she was smiling at him.

'Feeling better?' asked Nicholas.

'Much, much better. All I want to do now is to have Martin here, listening to that story. You both owe it to me.'

'Didn't you see Father again?'

'Never. I told your horrible aunts that I would go and take the children. They said that if I went there would be a divorce, and I wouldn't have custody—a sweet word to a twenty-two-year-old mother—custody of the children. So I said goodbye to you, which wasn't so hard, because you preferred so many things to me, and to Martin, which tore my heart in two. If I could have brought myself—years and years later—to forgive your father,

43

the memory of what I felt on leaving Martin would have been enough to prevent me.'

'Couldn't you have waited and talked to Father and—'

'No, Nicholas, I couldn't. Tell me, please, where is Martin now? And what does he look like?'

'He's in Kent, or he was when I last heard from him. And he looks—well, he's always looked pretty much the same.'

'The same as what?'

'Oh, you'll see. You'll see him when you come and stay with me in London—if he doesn't come out and visit you as soon as he gets my letter telling him I've found you.'

'I don't ever want to see England again.'

'Nonsense, Mother darling.'

'It isn't nonsense. Nicholas, would you like coffee here, or inside where it's cool, or down on the lower terrace under the vines? Down there, Carlos.'

They rose, and Nicholas took her elbow and they walked together down the stone steps. A silver tray was put on to a table, and Lorna poured out coffee. Nicholas, seated sideways on a low balustrade, nodded up towards the house and gardens.

'This place,' he said. 'When did you come here?'

'Eight years ago. It's always belonged to my husband's family, the Salvadors. It should have gone to Juan, but his mother—she was a

44

widow—refused to see him after his marriage to me and left it to his cousin who is, so to speak, the next in succession. His marrying me, you see, made her certain that there had been something between us. She was wrong; we married because I was adrift—and he always had a feeling, to the end of his life, that he'd been responsible for all the trouble. He felt that he'd allowed his ignorance of English life and customs to ruin us both. I think he felt, in marrying me, that he somehow made amends. We weren't in love, but we were happy, in a way, and we grew happier as time went on. He wasn't like your father; he was gentle and considerate and—and in an odd way grateful because we grew to be so happy. But his mother never forgave him. She was a virago, so I don't think he minded not seeing her, but he was born in this house, and he loved it and felt desperately sorry about never being able to come and live here.'

'Then—?'

'It's a sad story. The family priest was with my husband when he died, and when he came back to this house to see my mother-in-law, he convinced her at last that her son had done nothing wrong. He made her see and acknowledge the truth—and she did see, and she did acknowledge. She sent for me to tell me so, but before I could get down here she had died. She left me the house for my lifetime. I wasn't greatly interested then; I had a nice house in Madrid, and I had no intention of leaving it and coming to live in the south. But I had to come down here to clear up several things, and I was interested in seeing the house that Juan had loved so much. So I drove down. It was February and Madrid was bitter, bitter, bitterly cold. I wasn't driving myself and I dozed somewhere on the road. When I opened my eyes—we were just slowing down—there was the high pink wall and the huge doors and the iron gates and the view through them and—'

'You needn't go on,' said Nicholas. 'I looked through the iron gates, too. Did you stop to pick oranges?'

'No. I've got more soul than you. I was in a state of enchantment; I could only *feel*.'

'And so you stayed.'

'No, I didn't, not then. I came back later and I've lived here ever since, but I have to go away from time to time because there are things I can't leave. My orphanage.'

'Your—?'

'I had to have something to make up for you and Martin. I thought orphans would be the best. I had money, I had leisure, but I had no children. My children had been torn from me. They, too, were virtually orphans; they had no mother and a father who was no father. So I took up orphans.'

'I see. How many orphans?'

'Fifty-two in Madrid and thirty in Málaga. I

46

couldn't afford any more. Orphans cost a good deal. And whenever we get one whose name we aren't quite sure of, we name him Nicholas or Martin.'

'And if he's a she?'

'She's Nicholas or Martin, too. You shall see them one day. They're very, very sweet, and they're all very, very happy. And they make me happy, too. Without them I think I would have died. And it would have been your father's fault. You see that, don't you?'

'Clearly.'

'Good. Tell me, Nicholas, how could you turn out so nice when those horrid women brought you up?'

'They didn't. We saw them frequently, but we didn't live at Wychall for some time afterwards, as I told you. When you abandoned us, we—'

'Nicholas, if you ever, *ever*'

'When we abandoned you, we were sent down to old Cousin Georgina in Devon.'

'The little white house with roses?'

'No roses. I mistook the trellis for one of those solid, gymnasium ones. No more roses.'

'But Georgina—yes, she would be all right.'

'She was wonderful. Martin and I used to keep waiting lists of all the chaps at school who wanted to come home with us for the holidays. She was tall and severe and had a terrible tongue when you did anything you shouldn't have done, but she was fun, and the house was

47

fun, and the grounds were magnificent—trees and rabbits and moles. We had dogs and horses and a slope at the back that made the most dangerous toboggan run in the district. And a strawberry bed that stretched from that lemon tree to that lizard over there. And lashings of cream, and a cook that allowed you into the kitchen to see everything going on.'

'Did you miss me?'

'Every moment,' said Nicholas, and grinned at her.

'You didn't bully Martin, did you?'

'You can't bully Martin. He lives far away in a private world of his own, and he doesn't often leave it.'

'What's in it?'

'Well, he—It's difficult to explain, but you'll see.'

'See what?'

'He's got a sort of bee in his bonnet. He's only got one idea. Ever since he was chucked out of his prep school, he—'

'Ch-chucked—'

'Yes. Oh, it was nothing that need make you look like that. He's all right. He's just got this—this sort of kink, that's all. When you try to explain it, it makes people think he's on the sissy side, which he isn't. So I don't say anything, and people find out for themselves.'

'But surely, to me, his mother, you can try to—'

'Well, yes. Only, as I said, it sounds peculiar

48

when you say it out loud, and it gives people an entirely erroneous idea. However, as near as I can, I'll explain. He—Mother, there's a policewoman approaching.'

'A—?'

'A militant-looking female with a seven-league stride. Terrifying expression. She must be—'

'Oh, that's my secretary.'

'*Secretary*? Mother, she was born to brandish weapons. She can't possibly write letters!'

'No,' said Lorna in a resigned tone, 'she can't.'

CHAPTER FOUR

Florence van Leyte was delighted with Nicholas, delighted with the turn of events, and charmed, above all, with her own part in uniting mother and son. The uncomfortable feeling she had entertained on the score of being responsible for Stephanie's arrival and continuing presence in the house, no longer troubled her. If she had brought Stephanie, she had made handsome amends by bringing Nicholas to the Casa de Nuestra Señora del Carmen.

Having congratulated herself on presenting Lorna with a son, she began to ponder upon another aspect of the situation.

'How,' she enquired of her hostess, 'how could you have lived with me for so long without my finding out about your past?'

'You didn't ask,' said Lorna.

'Well, no,' said Florence. 'I shouldn't have asked in any case, but if I'd imagined that there was anything to find out, I shouldn't have *rested*. In all my experience, Lorna—and it's been considerable—I never saw a woman who looked less likely to be leading a double life.'

'I didn't live them both together.'

'To think of you as the mother of two sons. And I always thought you'd kept your figure because you didn't have children. I didn't have children, and I didn't keep my figure either, but that's neither here nor there. You look essentially a one-life, one-husband woman. Tell me, was he a brute?'

'Certainly,' said Lorna. 'Do you imagine that any of it was my fault?'

'Of course not. Did he beat you?'

'Well, he wasn't there, most of the time.'

'Oh, he neglected you?'

'He practically deserted me,' said Lorna.

'Was he handsome, like Nicholas?'

'Nicholas looks exactly like me, Florence.'

'Well, his chin doesn't. Is that dad's?'

'Yes. But Roderick had the chin without the other softening features.'

'Roderick! Did he ever try to patch things up?'

'There was no question of patching. Everything fell completely to pieces.'

'And then you married Salvador?'

'Yes.'

'Well, I don't know the rights and the wrongs of it, but I can't pretend that I'm sorry you ended up in this house. Lorna—'

'Well?'

'Now that I've put you so much in my debt by uniting you and Nicholas, I don't feel quite so bad about other things.'

'I hadn't noticed you feeling bad.'

'There's a story about a Spartan boy—I think it was a Spartan boy—who had things chewing at him and kept them under his hat.'

'Not his hat, Florence.'

'That's neither here nor there. What I'm saying is that now I don't feel so bad about Stephanie.'

'Were you—?'

'I didn't let you see because it was no use depressing you, but I wish I'd never had anything to do with bringing her here. She's probably got her fascination for those who like their women big and bossy, but let's both be honest and admit she's a washout.'

'Well, she's—'

'A washout. But the point is that she isn't the kind of girl you can just hand her hat and her paycheque, and anyhow she doesn't have a paycheque and there was our first big mistake. If you don't give them any pay, it makes it all

51

the harder to give them the push. I can't see how we can get rid of her until the summer, when we can just say we're both going away and shutting up the house. But summer's not here and Stephanie is, and I don't know how much longer you can bear it.'

'She doesn't worry me. I can't say I give her many letters—you can't write to old friends in the stilted kind of language she uses. I let her do the business ones, and she's not bad at those. I sign, and she takes them to the post herself; she says she doesn't trust the Spanish servants.'

'Well, Lorna, you may think I didn't know what I was doing, but when I was with her parents I got the idea that she was small and soft and sweet. She went to that wonderful school, and her mother showed me a whole cabinet full of prizes.'

'She got them all on Sports Day. She can run very fast.'

'Well, could I guess they were all for the egg-and-spoon race? I thought they were for reading and writing. She went straight from there—at her own request, her mother said—to a place where they taught you how to pound a typewriter. She sounded the nice, quiet, student type. Then she met this Sven and they made it sound as though he'd taken one look and bowled right over. Now I can see what really happened. That poor boy's on the run, but what can you do against a girl who was the champion sprinter of St Whowasit's? I only hope he gets away. If he knows what's good for him, he'll stay with the whales. At least they won't squint at him and say in that upstage voice, 'Thart is the kind of thing I kennot tolerate.'

'Florence, you'll hurt your larynx.'

'I have hurt it. What were we saying about your first husband?'

'About how awful he was and how lucky I was to be out of his clutches, and how happy I am now.'

She was very happy. The only cloud in her sky was the dismaying realization that Nicholas could not tell his superior officers that, owing to an unexpected increase in his family, he would be unable to see more of them until the *Panther* sailed. It had been a further disappointment to realize that a ship in process of being refitted was not one to which she could be invited in order to familiarize herself with this hidden side of Nicholas' existence. She could—and did—throw the house open to his friends, but she would have liked to go aboard the *Panther* and see that her son's surroundings were such as would afford him maximum comfort while he was in pursuit of his duties. She went once or twice to Gibraltar at his request, but she disliked the Rock and its narrow, noisy streets, and Nicholas did not press her to go again. He concentrated, instead, upon issuing invitations to his mother's house on a carefully selective basis.

The Casa de Nuestra Señora del Carmen wasn't just a house, he argued; people would give their ears to get inside it. He had no use for their ears, but there were certain other things that might be useful. Most useful of all was the realization of what his mother's beauty and charm did to the autocratic gentleman who had hitherto been able to order his life— Lieutenant-Commander Tenterby. Life in the Navy, always pleasant, now became full of exquisite possibilities, all conducted on an agreeable, let-us-understand-one-another-as-gentlemen basis.

Lorna found it pleasant to sit on the terrace and listen to so many English voices once more. She was too lovely, too young, too rich not to have had her full share of homage. She had been offered many homes and many husbands in many lands, but her circle, though cosmopolitan enough, had been predominantly Spanish. Having thought of herself, for many years, as Spanish, she was surprised to find that the presence of so many Englishmen in her house gave her peculiar pleasure. She charmed everybody without effort; only to the officers in Nicholas' immediate circle did she feel bound to exert herself to please, and the effect was devastating. Nicholas saw strong men go down and made the most of their downfall. While others basked in the sunlight of his mother's presence, he made hay.

Lorna was grateful to him for his delicacy in putting aside, for a time, any mention of Carmela. He gave his mother, or it seemed to her that he gave her all his thoughts and all his affection. The relationship between them was so perfect that she sometimes found herself wondering whether eighteen years of separation were not worth while when at the end there was this exquisite sense of rediscovery. Nicholas was indeed her own son: they were so much alike that Florence, watching them, wondered why the resemblance had not struck her fully from the first. Nor was the resemblance in appearance only; Lorna found, to her delight, that she could enjoy her son's companionship and discover daily some fresh points of similarity between them; they thought alike; their outlook was, in essentials, the same, and in both of them love of laughter was almost their strongest characteristic. In Lorna, the laughter was lazy; in Nicholas, mischievous, but again and again their eyes met, laughter-filled, and then sobered and signalled a mutual congratulation on their meeting.

Her gratitude to him for his self-control took the form of reintroducing the subject of Carmela at the earliest opportunity, and the look on Nicholas' face led her to encourage him to talk of his love and his hopes whenever they were alone together.

He had not seen Carmela since his meeting

with his mother, but Lorna was in no doubt as to the news having reached the Fernandez. News was news, and in this country it spread itself; Don Manrique and his family would by now be well aware of the fact of her relationship to Nicholas. Lorna, brooding over the subject in her bedroom one morning, realized that their position would be an awkward one; it was one thing for Don Manrique to discourage a self-confident young foreigner who had had the impertinence to raise his eyes to his daughter; it was quite another to extend anything less than the maximum courtesy and encouragement to the son of Lorna Salvador, who was the daughter of Juanita Gamez del Ruiz y Lima, who had been the great friend and first love of Don Manrique's father. It made things difficult; from Don Manrique's point of view, it would make things a good deal worse.

She could spare little time, however, for Don Manrique this morning.

Nicholas was expected to lunch and Lorna, from her bedroom, heard the staccato splutter of his car and smiled at Consuela, who was helping her to change. Consuela was sixteen; she had once tended goats and had been promoted to the position of water-carrier at the Inn at Estronella. From there, by a process of study that consisted solely of staring into the bedrooms of interesting extranjeras, she had graduated to the position of lady's-maid to

Lorna. She had flashing black eyes, a profusion of long, black ringlets, and she was deeply in love with Nicholas. She heard his footsteps on the tiled corridor and threw open the door with a promptness and energy that was a welcome in itself. He entered, patted Consuela on the head and kissed his mother tenderly, and Lorna experienced again the sweet half-shyness that came over her whenever he swept in thus, before she was completely dressed.

He ignored the chair that Consuela pushed towards him, and sat on the bed, marring its smoothness considerably and doing further damage by pulling out the pillows and punching them until they made a comfortable rest for his head.

'I've news for you, Mama,' he stated, when he was settled.

'News? I suppose you've seen Carmela,' said Lorna.

'No. I'm going up there this afternoon. I've been feeling rather sorry for Don Manrique lately—be interesting to see how he's going to behave now that you're in the picture. I'll go up fairly late, I think, then they'll have to ask me to stay to dinner.'

'That'll make you very late back to Gibraltar, won't it?'

'Not too late.' He gave his mother an appreciative glance. 'Nice nylon things they produce nowadays, makes a nice change from the red flannel of your youth, darling,

57

doesn't it?'

'It does,' agreed Lorna equably. 'I think women's underclothing is very sensible nowadays.'

'Sensible? Nonsense, my sweet!' Nicholas spoke with energy. 'They're too silly for words. Women always tell you that if they designed houses and built them, they'd be much easier to work in than the ones that men have been designing all this time. It sounds a good story, but why don't they go ahead and take over the designing and building? Nobody's stopping them. Only you'll find that the results won't be as spectacular as they hope. Look at their underwear. They design that themselves, don't they? And you've only got to watch a woman, first thing in the morning, struggling into one of those uplift affairs, to size up what they'd do in other designing spheres. To hook the things up at all, they have to screw their arms behind them, and then they have to twist them up as far as their shoulder blades and then they have to grope for a hook one side and a home for it on the other. Nobody but a contortionist could do it, and yet I've watched all that writhing and—'

'I'd be glad to know when you watched this interesting process, Nicholas.'

'That, as Florence would say, is neither here nor there, darling. You're trying to hedge. The point is that women's clothes aren't as sensible as you said they were. They—'

'You've convinced me,' said Lorna. 'Now tell me your news.'

'It isn't good news. Marty's been chucked out again.'

Lorna turned and faced him with an exclamation of distress that made Consuela, who understood nothing of the conversation but who followed every shade of expression, look at her anxiously.

'Martin! Oh—What's happened, Nicholas?'

'Just the usual. This makes the fourth—no, fifth time. I imagine Father's purple with passion. He made a special effort last time to what he called meet Marty half-way and went to a lot of trouble to get him this job. He said he didn't understand Marty's aims and didn't want to, but as a father he felt that he must help him to settle down into something definite instead of ruining his career at the outset by—you know the sort of thing? I'm sorry for the old man. He's beginning to wonder whether one of his sons—not me, of course—hasn't got a quite serious kink. He's not a patient man, my papa. He's the kind of—oh, I forgot, darling, you've met him, haven't you?'

'Nicholas,' said Lorna with what, for her, was remarkable firmness, 'if you don't tell me at once, slowly and clearly, what it is that Martin gets thrown out for, I shall go mad.'

'I'm telling you. Marty's a one-idea man. His idea is so preposterous that it's difficult, as I explained to you, to tell people about it without making him out to be a fool. He's no fool. For years I've been torn between seeing his point and seeing Father's point. At the moment I'm rather more inclined to Father's point of view. He—'

'One moment,' said Lorna. 'Why do you call him Marty?'

'Prep school. There were three fellows with Martin for a surname, and there were no less than four Martin prefixes. Something had to be done, so they were all renamed. Martin became Marty and it stuck.'

'Why does he always get—'

'Chucked out?' Nicholas hitched himself up on his pillows. 'I'll tell you. It all began at that same prep school. It wasn't a bad place, but they were doing pretty well—too well—and I think, looking back, that they'd got too many boys. That made it necessary for every boy to do the same thing at the same time as all the other boys. That means that the fellow who falls out of line isn't popular with the authorities. Marty kept in line until our second summer term, when the school acquired an extra bit of ground and built a long line of form rooms facing the river. Between the river and the new building, they carved up the ground into small plots and gave each boy his own piece and told him to go ahead and make it bloom. Flowers, that was the idea. The strip was to be coaxed from a wilderness into a blaze of colour, all the result of the boys' loving care

60

and daily tending. It wasn't a bad idea, on the whole. It kept us out of doors and it gave the botanically minded a chance to watch things growing. Some of us enjoyed it and some of us didn't, but those who didn't managed to get someone else to tend their bit. I never touched my plot, but I got all the credit. But Marty—'

'Well?'

'It got him at a bad time. He'd collected a lot of pets—a mole, a ferret and a very young owl. Before the make-your-garden-grow era, he'd been ideally happy, spending all his spare time keeping his livestock going. He tried to farm out his garden, but he was in a batch of chaps who were pretty small—naturally—and who found digging and planting quite a heavy enough job on their own patch without taking on anybody else's. So Marty went on the dodge, and the school began to apply pressure. After all, it was only a smallish patch, and there was no question of his overdoing it. But he wouldn't co-operate, and so they started whittling down his beloved animals, until there was only the owl left. It was a mistake, of course, and very unenlightened, but they could hardly make one exception, I suppose, or the whole scheme would have fallen down. So Marty cooked up a scheme of his own. He thought out a way of having a garden without toil. He began to use his talent for drawing and painting. We all knew what he was doing, but it was such a new line in trying to do the authorities down, that nobody dreamt of giving him away. Marty planned, produced and planted a fake garden, and on Speech Day the local Duchess gave him a thump of congratulation on his lupins and handed him the prize. And all would have been well if she hadn't bent down to smell a rather lovely rose—and stood up again with her nose covered in two shades of pink paint.'

There was silence. Then Lorna drew a deep breath.

'Go on,' she said.

'That was chuck-out number one and it was spectacular. He moved on, and he did the same thing again—gratuitously. You see, by this time, he'd been caught with his own cheese. He'd started out to do the thing once, but he couldn't stop. There was no compulsory gardening now, but he found one of the junior resident masters whose garden didn't come up to the Head's idea of a well-kept frontage. Marty went to work. His equipment had grown and he could have produced a ready-made garden in a night, but he was growing cautious. He took a week and then made the mistake of leading the Head down the garden path and showing him a flourishing display of daffodils. You can't, you shouldn't show an intelligent headmaster daffodils in July. Daffodils are the flowers that bloom in the spring, tra-la. So that was the second chuck-out.

'Well, Father thought that his talent for reproducing life-like flowers on life-like stems was all very well as a rather eccentric hobby, but it was time Marty settled down to some legitimate money-earning profession, and so he approached a friend of his—a thing he didn't like doing at all—and he landed Marty the kind of job that most young men would have made a go of. But Marty stuck to his idea of gardens springing up overnight—and so he's out on his ear again, and I think he's making straight for Gibraltar.'

Lorna's eyes widened.

'You mean he's—'

'He wired me to say he was on his way.'

'But—' Lorna's face was blank with dismay. 'But Nicholas, I wrote to him. Just after you came here that first time, I sent him a letter.'

'I don't know whether he'll have got it or not. I wrote myself and told him all about you, but that could have missed him, too. Can I bring him straight out here when he arrives?'

'Oh, Nicholas!'

He looked at her expression and laughed.

'Now you're growing into a proper mama,' he told her. 'You look really worried. Take that furrow off your brow.'

'Will he come by air?'

'Air! My God, Mother, he'd need a plane of his own for all his equipment. No, he'll come by road. He houses all his stuff—he wouldn't be parted with it on any consideration—in a

63

sort of vehicle. He bought a jeep and an old milk van and mated them. The result's always causing traffic jams wherever he drives it.'

'Nicholas, you will bring him here as soon as he arrives, won't you? Tell him I'm—no, don't tell him anything. Just bring him.'

As soon as lunch was over, Nicholas drove his car down to the garage to avail himself of the services of his mother's chauffeur. Lorna heard the sound of the engine die away in the distance, but ten minutes later, hearing it again, walked out on to the porch to see what had brought Nicholas back.

The car that had stopped outside the house, however, did not belong to Nicholas. Lorna recognized it instantly; it was the result of the mating of the van and the jeep, and its owner was getting out, was standing beside it and peering about him through his spectacles. He had seen her; he was smiling at her; he was coming towards her, shyly and somewhat hesitatingly and with an access of colour that had not for a moment troubled Nicholas. He had come to a stop and was standing before her.

Lorna would have given worlds to be able to say something, but, try as she would, no words came. She was unable to move, even to the extent of putting out a hand to grasp his. She could only stand and look, and presently she was aware that tears were running down her cheeks and that Martin had produced a

64

dreadful handkerchief and was agitatedly seeking a clean spot on it and mopping gently at her face. She gave a sound between a laugh and a choke, and they looked at each other in a silence which neither, now, felt it necessary to break.

He was tall; as tall as Nicholas, but without any of his brother's width of shoulder. Here was no splendid physique. There was no suggestion of muscle, no healthy tan. Martin was fair, with light-brown hair which was too long and which fell untidily over his forehead. His glasses were crooked and tied with string. His coat was torn in places, his trousers deplorable, his shirt a greyish-white. His face, boyish, appealing, was too thin; his eyes were grey, like his father's, but had none of his father's cool and confident look. His expression was at once shy and eager, and his manner faltering.

'Martin,' said Lorna at last.

He gave her a slow smile.

'Nick said you were lovely. Did you mind my c-coming?'

There was a suspicion of a stammer, but Lorna felt that this might be only shyness.

'Nicholas said you were going to join him,' she said.

'Not him; you, if you don't mind,' said Martin simply.

This time she was able to grasp his hand.

'Oh, Martin,' she said. 'I—you—Are you

really, really here to—to stay?'

'If you'll have me,' he said. 'Will my things be in the way?'

'There's unlimited room,' she said. 'You shall see and choose. You—' She broke off as Florence, unable to contain herself any longer, came out and joined them. 'Oh, Florence, this is Martin. Martin, here's Mrs. van Leyte, who's staying here.'

'Indefinitely,' said Florence. 'I hope I'm not butting in, I just happened to be passing and—' She stopped and studied Martin with small, keen twinkling eyes. 'Lorna,' she ended, 'I think he looks very nice.'

'I'm very glad to be here,' said Martin.

'Did you drive all the way from England without stopping?' enquired Florence. 'You look kind of dusty.'

'I came pretty f-fast. I didn't stop to make proper arrangements about the kind of m-money I'd need on the way.'

'Well, you look hungry,' said Florence. 'Lorna, why don't you look after your children properly?'

'She's wonderful,' said Martin.

'That's neither here nor there,' said Florence. 'She shouldn't keep you out here, talking. She should take you straight in and feed you.'

'I was just going to,' said Lorna. 'Martin, are you hungry?'

'As a matter of fact, I'm s-starving,' he said.

66

'What did I tell you?' said Florence. 'This way, Martin.'

CHAPTER FIVE

'But you see, Mother,' he said, over the remains of the meal, 'it isn't that I don't want to do whatever I have to do. It's just that I forget what it is for the m-moment and start working on my stuff. All I want to do is pass it on to someone who's interested and who believes in it, but, of course, n-nobody is, or does. The only people I run up against are the people who like to grow their gardens the h-hard way. And of course they think that the idea of an artificial garden positively s-stinks. I'd like to get hold of somebody who loathes gardening as much as I do, but who goes on scratching and s-scratching, evening after evening after a day's work, trying to produce gardens that'll do them c-credit. There was one. I went up and tackled him and asked him if he enjoyed gardening, and he said—well, what he said was rather strong.'

'We're not squeamish,' said Florence.

She was aware that a woman of feeling would have gone away and left Martin and his mother alone, but Martin, from her first glimpse of him, had made a curious impression on what she felt, uncomfortably, must be her heart. She could feel an unaccustomed melting round it, and she feared the worst. She had never in her life understood what was meant by the maternal instinct, but now, she told herself morosely, she was beginning to know only too well. If she knew anything, that peculiar feeling she was experiencing was going to get worse. A lot worse. She, Florence Undine van Leyte, who had kept her emotions in their place for over fifty years, was going to lie awake worrying about a thin slice of young man who didn't know enough to get his hair cut or remember which day the laundryman called. There was a hole in the sole of one of his shoes, she had seen it when he curled his feet round the legs of one of Lorna's beautiful chairs. His cheeks were hollow and his wristbones stuck out and he had beautiful teeth and a mouth which, if she didn't watch out, she would call mobile. Mobile! Oh God, Florence, remember who you are, and pull yourself together and listen to what he's saying about his ruling passion.

'I found,' said Martin, 'that he loathed every minute he spent in gardening, but he had to keep it at least tidy, because his neighbours were all gardening m-madly and producing roses in front and marrows at the back, and they d-despised him for not doing the same. What's more, if he let his grass grow long, or if he let his weeds get too weedy, the seeds would blow into the other gardens and wreck all that hard work and they'd all be after his b-blood. So instead of reading a paper of an evening, or taking his wife to the cinema, which he wanted to do, there he was grubbing in the ground. Him—and thousands like him. Think!' said Martin, leaning forward and planting an elbow in to a plate before Carlos could snatch it away. 'Just think! A garden and no grubbing. Gardening is for those who want to do it. Out here, it's different—you live in the sunshine, and flowers grow up before they're asked. You don't have to stir a f-finger. But at home, where a well-kept garden is a mark of respectability, where the man who can't or won't produce one loses c-caste, there ought to be a way of being able to get a ready-made garden if you want one. I—'

'Darling, just a moment,' put in Lorna, gently. 'Your coffee. Here, or—'

'Lorna, he'll have it here,' said Florence firmly. 'I want to hear about this ready-made system. I'm no gardener, and what's more, I don't like gardeners. A garden's like a pet dog—you can't leave it without worrying your inside out. You try and get an Englishwoman with a garden to do a trip with you and what do you get? She can't leave in autumn, because of the chrysanthemums; she can't leave in spring, because—oh Florence! you have no idea of how the daffodils look outside the dining-room window. She won't leave in summer, naturally, because it's going to be a good year

69

for strawberries, and she'll have to be there to bottle the gooseberries. Why don't you just take her and chain her by the leg to her favourite apple tree? There's no difference; she's rooted.'

'Florence, Martin wants to talk.'

'I know. I'll stop in a minute, Lorna, but I'm all wound up. I was just telling him that I understood what he means, much better than you do. I'm not tradition-tied and half of you is. Now Martin, go ahead and tell me how you fix these ready-mades.'

'It's very simple,' said Martin. 'It's merely— Would it be too much t-trouble to come outside and look?'

'Your coffee, Martin.'

'Later, Lorna,' said Florence. 'Come on outside.'

'It's simply this,' said Martin, from the depths of the truck. 'No, don't come in, I'll bring them out. Now this, you see, is the stem on which all flowers go. They're different sizes, according to the kind of flower you're going to put on them, and they're as strong as steel, and they'll stand any amount of hard b-buffeting. Perhaps I could put it into the ground and let you see. Yes, there. Now feel that.'

They felt it.

'Now we'll take a couple of spring flowers—I—'

'Snowdrops and daffodils,' said Florence.

'All right. I'll get them out—there. Now you

70

see? You screw whatever flower you want firmly into the stems, it takes a few seconds, that's all. I've done a lot of experimenting with the right textures and colours, but most of them look almost better than the real thing, now, and all of them are rain-, wind-, ice- and snow-proof.'

'In an English spring,' said Florence, 'they'd have to be.'

They stood for some time in silence, looking down at a row of snowdrops and daffodils blooming, incongruously, somewhat flamboyant. The delicate waxen and golden petals looked somewhat out of place, but of one thing there was no doubt whatsoever: they looked real.'

'I think they're lovely,' said Lorna, slowly. 'I—'

'If you use the word nature,' said Florence, 'I shall be very angry with you. Nature, nature, nature. How much is natural nowadays? Look at my hair! Look at everybody's teeth! Martin, next time a woman calls your flowers artificial, ask her how many perms she has a year. And if a man ups and says anything about nature, remember that he's probably talking through a whole set of gold or porcelain, and take no notice. Nature! What's natural about one of those gardens full of heart-shaped flower beds and fish ponds and yew walks and—well, what's natural about a flower bed, anyway? Formal garden—it speaks for itself. Nature!'

'Florence, darling, you're shouting.'

'I am?'

'Yes. But it's on Martin's behalf, and we're very grateful.'

'Martin,' demanded Florence, turning to him, 'how many of those flower set-ups have you got?'

'How many? Oh, just enough for d-demonstration purposes,' said Martin.

'But aren't you going to produce them? Put them on the market? Advertise them?'

'G-good heavens, no,' said Martin.

'And why not?' enquired Florence.

'Because I'm not interested in any of that k-kind of thing. All I want to do is to find a few people who'll agree that the thing's workable, that's all.'

'But that isn't all,' insisted Florence. 'You've got to find someone who won't only believe in it, but who'll go a whole lot further. You want someone—some hard-headed businessman who can take it up and—and launch it.'

'Well—no,' said Martin 'All I want is—'

'An interested partner who'd push it.'

'I don't see it as a big-business p-proposition,' said Martin mildly.

'Perhaps not; you've just been going at it from an artistic point of view, getting all those things painted and ready. But I think I've got a scheme.'

'No, Florence,' said Lorna firmly. 'No more schemes.'

'All I'm trying to do is get hold of a fellow with money and the brains to see that there's a future in this thing.'

'Well, if Martin wants money, I'll give it to him.'

'But you can't start him up in business with just money. You want a—a promoter.'

'No, honestly, I don't,' said Martin.

'Well, it won't hurt to ask somebody's advice. Somebody with force. A kind of what they call dynamic personality.'

She was silent, and her two companions saw clearly that she was calling dynamic personalities to mind. The pause lengthened, and Florence strove, but no forceful friends leapt into her memory. There was Woolly, of course, but that was absurd. There must be a lot of men she knew who would. It was a great pity she'd let all those friends of both her husbands slip away unnoticed. Any one of them would have—but they had melted into the past, taking their names and addresses with them. Perhaps Woolly could be built up a little. After all, if she said he was dynamic, nobody here could come right out into the open, after they'd seen him, and actually prove that he wasn't. Woolly would have to do. There was nobody else, and she was going to help Martin, whether he wanted her to or not. She would bring Woolly, she decided recklessly, and leave the rest to God.

'I've got the very man,' she announced. 'He's

73

in France at this moment, and I can get hold of him and ask him to come right along and talk to Martin.'

'No, Florence,' said Lorna.

'There's no harm in just talking, is there?' pleaded Florence.

'It's just that Martin doesn't—'

'And he's my brother,' begged Florence. 'Don't you want to see my brother, Lorna?'

Lorna hesitated, trying to find a polite form of refusal, and as she waited, Nicholas drove up from the garage, brought his car to an abrupt stop and stared at his brother.

'H-hello, Nick,' said Marty.

'Well, well, well, well,' said Nicholas. 'Mother, what did I tell you?'

'H-homing instinct,' explained Martin.

'Good for you,' Nicholas clapped him on the back with pleasure. 'And now that you're here, I think maybe I can use your help. Are you still as good as you used to be at distracting the attention of parents from their cherished offspring. . . .' Nicholas's voice faded away as he drew his brother into the house.

Lorna stared after them, lost in a daze of happiness.

'And now you and I, Lorna,' Florence said, 'will go and write that letter.'

'What letter?' asked Lorna in surprise.

'Why, the letter to my brother, asking him to come. Don't you remember? You asked me to ask him.'

CHAPTER SIX

Such was the force of Florence's phraseology, that before a week had gone by, a gentleman called Woolly Estwood drove up to the entrance of La Casa de Nuestra Señora del Carmen and there found himself held up by a small boy who peered through the eyehole in a manner denoting the deepest suspicion and distrust.

There was nothing about Mr. Estwood's conveyance that gave reassurance. Strange vehicles had lately come to the Casa. There had been the small, spluttering affair of Don Nicholas, and the odd, clumsy affair of Don Martin, but this—of all strange affairs, this was the strangest.

Woolly's lumbering equipage had an engine whose name commanded respect throughout the world, and which had given him several years of trouble-free travel. But, as the engine had been chosen to give the best service, the coachwork had been designed to afford Woolly something more than a space for himself and his luggage. It was less a car than a home; a canvas-covered waggon in which he could eat and sleep and live in the style to which he was accustomed. He could work in it, or he could relax; he could have coolness in hot weather and a stove when it was cold. But these

75

were amenities which any tent or caravan might have afforded. Woolly's waggon offered far more: a long, folding pier from which he could fish; an observation platform from which he could take his bearings if ever he lost them; most dear to his heart, and affording the most value to spectators, was the large canvas swimming bath which trailed behind and into which Woolly could pump water for a bath if he was ever disposed to take one. Others might choose to share the sea with the sharks, or the river with the crocodiles; in his bath of canvas, pointed out Woolly proudly, a man could swim in safety, if he could swim.

Such was Woolly's travelling home, and it is small wonder that the custodian at the Casa del Carmen, peering out, found himself too paralysed to perform his duties.

'Hey!' called Woolly mildly, after a time. 'Open up there, sonny.'

'Quién es?' asked the gate-keeper, removing an olive stone for greater clarity of utterance, and then replacing it in his mouth.

'It's me,' explained Woolly. 'Now you stop peeking through that hole and let down the drawbridge, son. I'm here to see the Señora.'

'Señora?'

'That's it, you've hit it first time. The Señora van Leyte. Come on, now.'

'No se.'

The grille closed with a snap. Woolly, opening what on a more conventional vehicle

76

would have been a door, got out and tested the might of his fist against the portals. Finding that the portals had the best of it, he went back again, took out a newspaper from a shelf behind him and settled down with the patience that was one of his strongest characteristics.

A twitter, a chatter on the other side of the wall told him that his case was being discussed. The grille opened, and a small girl peered at him and studied him intently.

'Human,' explained Woolly.

The grille closed and opened again. A man looked through and spoke in rapid and—to Woolly—unintelligible phrases.

'Take your time,' invited Woolly, in a long-drawn-out, nasal drawl. 'I'm not in a hurry. I didn't want to come in the first place, but Flo wants something, and she sounds like she wants it badly. I don't know what it is she wants me to do, but I'm here to do it. She said she'd be mad at me if I didn't do it. But if you don't let me in, I guess that lets me out.'

An idea came to him suddenly, and the fact that it had come and that it was a good one, kept him silent with wonder for a time. Then he took a small notebook from his pocket and tore a page from it. Scrawling his name on the paper, he got out and pushed it through the grille.

'I don't have my visiting cards on me, hombre,' he said. 'You take that along to the selection board and see what they make of it.

I'll just stay out here, and thanks for the welcome.'

He went back to his waggon once more; a long, lean, straggling man of about fifty-five, with a face not unlike his sister's, except for the eyes. Woolly's were blue and bland and rather beautiful, pools that reflected light, but little else. They were on his newspaper, calm, placid. There might be questioning and fuss and flutter within the Casa del Carmen, but on Woolly's side of the wall all was tranquil.

The face of a plump young woman appeared at the grille, and white teeth flashed a reassuring signal. There was a grinding noise, and Woolly looked up from his paper to see the great doors opening.

'You see,' said Florence, standing beside Lorna on the steps of the porch, 'that's Woolly all over. You mention business, and he's with you before the ink's dry.'

She spoke with an assurance that masked a horrid gnawing of anxiety. He had come; that meant that he had taken in at least the gist of the letter. She had told him not to come in his contraption, but that had been hoping too much.

'He must have more confidence in your schemes than I have,' said Lorna, smiling.

'Lorna, is that kind?' demanded Florence.

'Well, then, he must admire you very much.'

'Admire!' Florence was surprised into frankness. 'He's never admired a woman in his

78

life, he's just not—' She stopped and substituted a sentence hastily. 'All he's got is a good business sense. He doesn't waste time once he's seen the possibilities of a good business deal. Force and drive, as I told you.'

Lorna might have answered, but at that moment she was too busy staring at a stove chimney that had appeared among the trees and was moving slowly towards them. Before her astonishment could find expression, the purr of a thorough-bred engine was heard, and Woolly's mobile came into view and approached the porch. A wild shriek from Florence proclaimed her certainty that the chimney was about to crash into the porch roof, but at that moment it folded back as neatly as the funnel of a steamer going under a bridge, and Woolly drew up before them.

Lorna, watching him climb out awkwardly and come towards her, found herself wondering where he got his name. Woolly was clearly not a term that could be applied to his pate, which was almost innocent of wool. It could not describe his clothing, which was of heavy cotton, and in this climate it could scarcely apply to his underwear. His wits, Florence had assured them, were the sharpest in all Canada. If she had not done so, one might have wondered a little. Shelving the problem, Lorna held out a hand and uttered a conventional greeting, and Woolly, making the sternest effort of his life, muttered something in reply and then relapsed into a coma.

He was not feeling very well, for too much had happened to him within the past four minutes. He had been outside the gate, a free and happy man, caring little whether he was admitted or not. He had driven in, to be faced by a second gate and to glimpse through it a scene of such enchantment as to make him forget who he was and why he had come. Being a simple man, he assessed what he saw in terms of dollars and felt himself turning pale. He slowed down almost to walking pace and crept reluctantly round the side of the house, and there the glory of the view brought him to a dead stop. A glimpse of his sister standing awaiting him had a sobering enough effect to make him finish the journey and apply the chimney-folding mechanism in time; then he looked out and saw Lorna, and was lost.

She was in blue—a tender blue that reminded Woolly of cornflowers and recalled, for the first time for forty years, the colour of his mother's Sunday dress. The eyes he looked into smiled a soft welcome; a lovely form swayed towards him and he heard a voice that made him think of the brooks beside which he loved to halt and spend quiet nights.

Lorna was familiar with the symptoms and knew that she could do nothing for Woolly, as she had been unable to do anything for his predecessors. Florence saw his plight and was plunged into despair. Other men saw Lorna and fell into a trance, but they retained enough intelligence to enable them to think, however dimly, of other matters. Woolly's case was different; his mental equipment, Florence admitted unhesitatingly, didn't stretch to more than one thing at a time. For the moment he was beyond her influence; until he recovered, any attempt at intelligent conversation with him would be a waste of time.

The question of accommodation for the visitor offered no difficulty; Woolly refused steadfastly to live in the house. If he could be allowed, he said, to drive his waggon down there, somewhere near the water, he would be happy, and he would look after himself in the way he was used to do. Martin drove away with him to choose a site, and they chose one which hid the stove-pipe effectively from the view of those up at the house. Woolly then proceeded with preparations for a meal, refusing Martin's offer of help, so Martin sat on the ground, leaned against a tree and became an interested onlooker. In between dives into the interior of his waggon, Woolly glanced surreptitiously at his companion and thought him a pleasant-looking young man. This was the one Florence had written of; this was the subject of that long, unintelligble letter. He was also—he was her son, and he, Woolly, was prepared, under those circumstances, to go to any lengths if by doing so he could please her. Woolly's spirits rose a little; he told himself that it looked as though he might, for once in his life, be in a position to please everybody: Lorna would be pleased if he helped her son, Florence would be pleased if he helped this young man, and the young man looked as though he'd be easy to please.

'Odd chap, that Woolly,' commented Martin, when he was alone with his mother. 'He's rigged up a wonderful outdoor kitchen out there. Looks as though he's going to roast an ox.'

'He isn't the sort of man I'd imagined he would be,' said Lorna. 'Didn't Florence say he was full of things like drive and energy?'

'Human dynamo, those were her words. And drive! Did *you* see any drive?'

'I can't say I did,' said Lorna. 'But I like him.'

'So do I. To tell you the t-truth, I was rather dreading it. I thought he'd come b-bouncing in and try to talk me into something. He's a happy sort of chap, Mother; you should go down and have a look at him. Gives you a feeling you've gone back a long way, to those books about pioneer trails; he looks as though he's just setting out at the head of an endless column. I sat there enjoying it. You really ought to go see.'

'I will,' said Lorna. 'Why didn't you have to wait at the gate, incidentally, Martin? I was in the middle of apologizing to Florence's
82

brother when it suddenly struck me that you came in without any trouble. How was that?'

'There was a slight hitch,' admitted Martin, 'until I put my face close to the little look-out and said my name was Saracen. That opened the gate so fast that I nearly fell t-through it.'

'Ah!' said Lorna. 'That would explain it. Since Nicholas came, there's been a lot of heartbreak on the estate over Señor Saracen. I suppose the name's a password now. Martin'—her voice became brisk—'didn't your father ever complain about the way you look?'

'I rather think he did,' said Martin, after consideration. 'Funny thing—I was thinking about him last night. I was wondering what he'd t-think of my being here.'

'Did you tell him you were coming?'

'I didn't exactly t-tell him. I sent him a postcard from some place or other on the way here. I said I was going to look you up. Tell me—'

'Tell you what?'

'Couldn't you make it up, or something? After all, it all happened an awfully long time ago!'

'So long,' said Lorna, 'that I've forgotten all about it. And so long, that it isn't worth digging up again and patching up. No. I'm not going to say anything against him, because he is, after all, your father, but I really don't care for people who cling to their own opinions like

83

bull-terriers and who haven't the elements of tact or consideration or sympathy or even humour. If you like those enormous, unyielding men with that rather brute strength, as it were, your father certainly fills the bill. I can't bear people who bulldoze their way through everybody else's feelings, but you do owe him a certain loyalty, and I hope you'll always remember that. Only you must allow me to have my own opinion, which is that he's a big bully.'

'He's not a bad-looking fellow, in a way,' commented Martin. 'But he's never—since I was old enough to j-judge, anyhow—shown any interest in women. Nick and I often wonder why he didn't marry again.'

'He only married me because I was too young to know what I was doing. No woman who had any sense would take him on for a single moment.'

'Oh, I don't know. I've seen one or two of them making quite distinct p-passes.'

'Passes?'

'Yes. There was one with rather attractive hair—you know the sort you drag back and have in a bun behind?'

'I can't say I care for the style.'

'On some women it's rather distinctive. You have to have the features, but this one certainly had them.'

'Really?'

'Yes. And she gave one l-look at Father—

this was when we stopped for petrol once—and she pretended she'd stopped her car too close to ours, and got out to see if she'd scratched our paint.'

'I hope your father scratched hers.'

'Oh, he knew what she wanted. He wasn't very forthcoming, but she dropped her address very casually into the conversation, and I often wondered afterwards if his stand-offish attitude was just for my benefit, and if afterwards he went and—'

'If he wants to look up every stray creature who—'

'Well, I don't say he did. But as Nick says, he's a man you c-can't overlook, and there's a sort of bull look about him that made us wonder whether—'

'Whether what?'

'Er—oh nothing,' said Martin. 'Mother, this is a wonderful place. How can you get used to living here in this loveliness?'

'I don't live here all the time,' smiled Lorna. 'I have to go to Madrid—I still have a house there, you know. I didn't imagine I'd ever come to regard the Casa del Carmen as my home, but each year, when I come back to it, I feel more and more that I don't want to leave it again.'

'Pity there weren't any Salvador sons,' commented Martin. 'Who does it go to?'

'It goes to somebody called Inez Salvador, who's the widow of somebody called Paco Salvador, who was first cousin to my husband,

Juan Salvador.'

'Seems funny to hear you say "my husband" like that,' said Martin thoughtfully. 'Was he a nice chap?'

'Very nice.'

'Did you ever miss Father?'

'No.'

'He's not a bad c-chap either, you know.'

'I haven't a word to say against him.'

Martin smiled. 'Nick said—'

'Well, what did he say?'

'Perhaps I shouldn't tell you. He said that it was a good thing to let you get it all off your ch-chest. He said you'd been saving it up, and it was much healthier to let it all come.'

'Oh, he did?'

'Yes. He's a good chap, isn't he?'

'I think he's wonderful. I think you're both wonderful. I can't imagine how I lived without you.'

'Why didn't you have any children—the second time, I mean?'

'I don't know. Perhaps because it was a rather half-hearted marriage. He was in love with someone else, and I was hurt and bewildered and lost.'

'Doesn't sound like you, somehow—hurt and bewildered and l-lost. I can't imagine you as anything but this—beautiful and sort of languid and laughing.'

'Did you ever miss me? Not me exactly, but just a mother?'

86

'Well, on Speech Days it would have been nice to have someone there.'

'Oh.'

'Nick and I never had anyone to show off. You'd have swept the b-board.'

'Thank you.'

'Mother, do you really think Mrs van Leyte meant what she said about her brother being here to talk business?'

'I'm only afraid she means a great deal more. When Florence wants to help anybody, she really lets herself go.'

'What I'd like,' said Martin, 'is a small bit of ground with a decent setting, fairly near London, where I can have a few exhibition gardens for people to come down and look at. Then they might see how easy it would be to have what looks like the real thing without any grind.'

'But if they liked what they saw, wouldn't they place orders, and if they placed orders, wouldn't you have to be in a position to supply what they want?'

'Well, there'd be t-time enough to think about that when somebody showed some enthusiasm. So far, people have just said that the idea's pre-preposterous and left it at that. How did this Florence come to live with you permanently?'

'She doesn't. It looks like that, but she hasn't really settled down here. She came with a letter of introduction from friends of mine in

Madrid, and I asked her to stay until she had completed the details of some trip or other that she wanted to do. Well, she stayed. When she'd been here for a while, she came to me and very sensibly and in quite clear language brought up the subject of money, and it ended by her making quite munificent donations from time to time to my favourite charities.'

'Your orphans?'

'Yes. And I've got some fallen women, too, and some nice old fishermen in a set of tiny houses on the coast about ten miles from here. Florence's cheques practically support them.'

'Will you ever get rid of Stephanie, do you think?'

'I don't see why not. She ought to be glad to move on; she rather disapproves of us all, I think.'

'Is Nick really serious about that Spanish girl?'

'Quite, quite serious. Have you ever been in love?'

'No. I'm not too keen on girls. Or perhaps I don't go down very well. Nick's got a certain t-technique, hasn't he?'

'He appears to have. Martin, when I was superintending your unpacking—'

'Funny. The school matron used to s-start off just like that.'

'I don't wonder. Martin, are those all the clothes you've got?'

'I've got an evening suit somewhere; I don't

think I brought it.'

'But shirts, socks, pyjamas?'

'Oh, I brought all *those*.'

'*All?*'

'I haven't bought much stuff lately. I suppose I've got a bit low.'

'Low! Martin, they're all in *shreds!*'

'Shreds?'

'Tatters.'

'Oh.'

'And, darling, they're not even *clean!*'

'What, really?'

'Can't you see when a thing's clean and when it isn't?'

'Well, yes. I always mean to go through the things, and then I start working and forget. There's no difficulty about a laundry here, is there? They t-take the stuff out and bang it on the stones, don't they?'

'Somebody has already been banging your stuff on the stones. They've banged it all to pieces. You've got to come shopping with me, Martin.'

'Oh, I say, not really?'

'And that hair—'

'Too long?'

'And your fingernails—'

'Too short?'

'And those glasses you wear, all stuck together with glue and string.'

'I meant to do something about them, but I don't think they're much good. I can see much better without them.'

'Then why do you wear them?'

'They said I had to.'

'*Who* said?'

'The school said.'

'But Martin, *which* school?'

'Prep school. They l-lugged me off to an oculist and he gave me glasses and said I was to keep 'em on.'

'B-but haven't you had a sight test since then?'

'Well, no.'

'You mean those are the glasses the oculist gave you when you were—how old?'

'Oh, tennish.'

'Ten! *Martin!* You—why, you might have been *blind* by now!'

'When I really wanted to s-see anything, I just took them off.'

'T-took them—' Lorna gave a sigh of hopelessness. 'Well it's too late to worry about that, but I'm certainly not going to leave your clothes in the state they're in. We're going into Málaga this afternoon.'

'Why not into Gib? Better tailors and some decent English shirts.'

'Very well. We'll go into Gibraltar. We'll try and get hold of Nicholas; he might be free for an hour or two.'

They did their shopping, and Martin managed to get a telephone call through to Nicholas, who met them and gave them tea.

Lorna, who had long since given up the tea hour, sat behind the unaccustomed equipment and poured out cup after cup for her sons and looked across the table at them with affection and some amusement.

'What's funny?' enquired Nicholas, through a muffling mouthful of chocolate cake.

'Nothing's funny. Don't talk and eat at the same time. I was just looking at you both, that's all. After all, I've got a lot of looking to make up, haven't I?'

'Would you have recognized us,' asked Martin, 'if you'd met us on the street somewhere?'

'Instantly.'

'How?'

'Instinct,' said Lorna, and heard Nicholas' shout of laughter. 'And other things, too,' she qualified. 'Your eyes. And I don't think boys change as much as girls do. Martin's hair grows in exactly the way it always did—straight up, and then falling over one eye unless it's well cut. And your chin, Nicholas.'

'It's Father's chin.'

'Yes. It's a pity, but you can't have everything. You've got some of my features.'

'And your nature. Marty hasn't, I warn you. He looks a good deal more pliable than I do, but just below the surface—and not always below, either—you come upon Father. Granite.'

'I don't like to be p-pushed round,' said

91

Martin mildly. 'People are always trying it.'

'I'm surprised you got him looking decent with so little difficulty,' said Nicholas. 'You've mesmerized him.'

'It wasn't all Mother,' explained Martin. 'It was the C-Casa de Nuestra Señora del Carmen. You can't walk round the C-Casa de Nuestra Señora del Carmen in torn trousers. Doesn't go, somehow. Nick, what about running up to see Carmela sometime soon? I'd like a drive up there. I'll keep mother and father busy while you talk to daughter.

'Carmela's parents,' pointed out Martin, 'can't be any s-stickier than the ones that girl had in Canterbury—what was her name?'

'Nobody,' said Nicholas, 'was ever interested in her name. And it's all dead mutton, anyway. This is something entirely different. Will you really take it on?'

'Of course I'll take it on. I'm at a bit of a loose end at the moment. That chap, Woolly, keeps looking at me as though he's going to say something, but nothing comes out. He's probably working out a scheme with his s-sister, so while they're at it, I'm at your whatsit—disposal.'

'Well, look here, I can get off day after tomorrow. I'll pick you up at about three and take you up to Carmela's.'

'I've got no S-Spanish, of course,' said Martin. 'That might hamper me a bit.'

'Don Manrique's English is quite sound,'

put in Lorna, 'so long as you keep to simple sentences. But his wife doesn't speak a word of any sort of English.'

'Well, it ought to be interesting,' said Martin. 'Day after tomorrow?'

'Three o'clock. Will you mind our leaving you, Mother, my pet?'

'I shall be relieved,' said Lorna.

'Then it's a date, Marty. We'll go up on Wednesday.'

They went up on Wednesday, and so it happened that Roderick Saracen, arriving by air at Gibraltar to speak seriously to his sons and to recall at least one of them into the sphere of his own influence, was informed that both gentlemen were to be found at the Casa de Nuestra Señora del Carmen.

And after an hour's reflection, Roderick, spurred by anger and a sense that he was being treated with gross unfairness, borrowed a car and drove out to prove to himself—and to anybody else who had any doubts about the matter—that he was still master of his own family.

CHAPTER SEVEN

Lorna was alone when he arrived. The boys were at Yago; Florence had taken her brother and Stephanie for a drive. She saw him as she came from the garden into the cool, dim hall. Her eyes were full of sunlight, and she was dreaming, and completely unprepared, but she needed only one glance at his figure, silhouetted against the strong sunlight as he stood under one of the arches of the porch, to be able to identify him instantly, and with an anger that shook her.

He had got in, unheralded, unannounced; how, she could not imagine, until she remembered that he would use the password and, as a Saracen, be at once admitted. She had been out in the garden; the servant who had been seeking her came in, and she waved him away. She turned, without a word, and led the way to the drawing-room, and Roderick followed her. They stood facing one another, and neither was in a hurry to speak.

They were both angry, but anger was giving way to surprise. Lorna had remembered his height and width, but she had not realized that the years would make him yet wider. She acknowledged, fairly and unreservedly, that he was a splendid-looking man; his eyes were as cool and level and steel-grey as she remembered them; his mouth was as firm and his expression as unreadable. His back was to one of the large windows and her eyes, glancing past the bulky form, rested for a moment on the outline of the Rock of Gibraltar, rising sheer and strong out of the blue water. They were the same, she thought, rugged,

94

immovable.

His thoughts were more confused. She had been—he could have sworn—smaller, and she had had a childish awkwardness and a manner rather like Martin's. There was no awkwardness now, and no shyness, and certainly no eagerness. And her figure—of course, it was not to be expected that it would be girlish still, but there had been no promise of this. She had worn well, by God, he thought, and the thought brought contempt. Luxuriously petted and protected from the dust of ordinary existence—yes, she would wear well. But she had turned from a pretty little girl into an outstanding-looking woman, and it was easy to see what effect she had had on her two sons.

'Well?' said Lorna, at last.

'Perhaps we'd better sit down,' he said.

'I'd rather stand, if you don't mind. I don't feel like sitting down. I feel rather angry, and very much surprised at seeing you in this house.'

'There's nothing to be surprised about,' he said. 'I've got two sons and they're both making fools of themselves. Did you think I'd sit there at home and let them both throw away good careers?'

'What did you think you could do by coming out here?'

'If you mean to this house, I can say at once that I hadn't the smallest intention of coming anywhere near it, or near you. I came here because it didn't look as though I could get hold of them anywhere else.'

'Martin is living here. I think he intends, for the moment, to go on living here. I'm his mother, you know.'

'Nothing of the sort,' he said flatly. 'You left them both in the lurch, and you've lived without them for eighteen years and more. There was nothing in the least maternal about that.'

There was a long pause during which Lorna fought, not for words, but for breath. For the first time in her life, she realized that to strike somebody was not an unwomanly action, as she had imagined hitherto; it was a need, a duty, the only effective answer to certain kinds of attack. Longing rose in her, and then her self-control returned and the moment passed.

Roderick, for his part, felt a great deal better. It was something to have drawn first blood. It was a good thing to have checked all that sort of thing at the outset. She asked for it; she got it.

'Leave my house,' managed Lorna at last.

That, at any rate, he reflected, was coming down to brass tacks. It was the level at which he liked to deal with all matters, business or domestic. She was at least being natural now, and that was going to save a lot of time.

'I'll leave in a moment,' he said. 'I've got one or two things to say first.'

'You've got nothing to say to me. You can say anything you wish to Nicholas and Martin in Gibraltar. They can visit me, stay with me, any time they want to, and I shall welcome them.'

'And encourage them to defy me.'

'Don't talk as though they were children. They're both grown men. Don't imagine that I shall interfere between you and them.'

'You've done pretty well already. What was all that rubbish you told Nicholas?'

'I don't understand you,' said Lorna, icily.

'You gave him an entirely garbled account of your reasons for leaving me.'

'I told him the facts.'

'He knows the only important fact: his mother got along without him for nearly twenty years. There's not much point in filling him up with a lot of overdue explanations.'

'I think it is. He understands a great deal more than he did.'

'All you gave him was your own version.'

'It was time he heard it.'

'You told him I was a monster.'

'Then I put it mildly.'

'The only monstrous act was yours, in leaving two young children, to say nothing of a husband.'

'A husband who had stated his intention of divorcing me for something I hadn't done; two children who would have been taken from me after the divorce.'

97

'Good God,' said Roderick, 'a man hears news about his wife that tears him to pieces, and he sits down and writes an impulsive letter. Is that a basis for abandoning a home and a husband and a family?'

'I didn't have a home. I lived with two horrid women who—'

'They thought the world of you. Being normal, decent Englishwomen and not excitable Spaniards, they didn't show it.'

'They watched everything I did and put the worst possible construction on it.'

'They were two perfectly pleasant, kind, good-hearted women who took an interest in you.'

'They read the worst into everything and told wicked lies about what they saw.'

'I would like you to know that both my sisters are dead.'

'Then they can hear everything I'm saying, and I hope they know now how wickedly they behaved. At least they must be aware, wherever they are, that it was all their fault in the first place. And they must know that they were wrong—wickedly, wickedly, wickedly wrong.'

'If they were, you could have told them so, instead of behaving like a persecuted heroine. You could have explained. But you preferred to let them believe the worst. And so, believing the worst, they wrote to me—kindly and with the best intentions.'

'And your letter to me, I suppose, was also kindly and with the best intentions?'

'I was demented, as any man would have been.'

'But you were convinced. Having married me out of my cradle, you—'

'You were seventeen and the daughter of a Spanish woman, and you were warm-blooded and passionate and a good deal safer married.'

'I had two children before I was twenty, and—'

'That's why I thought it wiser to stay abroad for a bit. I don't want to drag back things that are better left alone, but I'd like bare justice. You never gave me a chance. I wrote a letter when I was in a state bordering on madness, and you read it as a cold statement of intention. You behaved like a sulky schoolgirl. You were a grown woman, with responsibilities; you were a wife and a mother, and you walked out at the first spot of trouble that turned up. You could at least have stayed and put up a fight.'

'What for? For a man who doesn't know the meaning of the words trust, and faith, and understanding?'

'All right. I wrote in haste. But the haste was nothing to the haste with which you acted. I hurried home, and you were gone, and my sisters were demented with worry. I could understand—afterwards—how you could leave me, but I've never been able to understand how you could leave the children.

Never. Never. If I wasn't worth a struggle, surely they were? But you ran away in a temper, like a child.'

'I was a child.'

'No, you weren't; you liked to think of yourself as one, that's all. You merely built up a case for yourself. There was not a bit of malice in either Kate or Heloise; I had merely asked them to keep an eye on you.'

'They did.'

'But I hope you see now—because you can't bring up the excuse, any more, that you're a child—that you acted with, to say the least of it, insane rashness. You must admit that you would act more sanely now.'

'Would you write a letter like that now?'

'No. I don't mind going as far as to say I wouldn't.'

'Then I might act more sanely. But you were warped and insensitive, and you robbed me of my children.'

'And you're trying to do it again. That's why you're here.'

'I'm here—let me make this quite clear—to make those boys see reason. I know perfectly well that you're encouraging them both. You're doing your best to throw Nicholas and that girl together.'

'Certainly I am. You—without having set eyes on her—will be quite ready to take sides against her.'

'I've nothing against the girl. But do you

deny that her father's a smuggler?'

'Certainly I don't.'

For the first time there appeared a slight crack in the stony mask.

'You—admit that?'

'Of course he's a smuggler! How do you think he got rich so quickly? It wasn't his farm or his olives or his cork trees.'

'Smuggling!'

'A harmless sport in these parts. A few commodities out of Gibraltar into Spain, along the coast or over the mountains. Tobacco and perhaps spirits and medicinal supplies and not, as you probably imagine, opium and worse. Kipling told you all about it: "brandy for the parson, 'baccy for the clerk." Why don't you do as he advised and watch the wall while the gentlemen go by?'

'Smuggling! Nicholas with a father-in-law who's a notorious—'

'He's not at all notorious. You've been reading too much sensational literature. He organizes a few meeting points; he rides out with a few friends on a dark night and makes the Guardias Civiles look even sillier than their silly hats do. You'd better rid your mind of any ideas of anything sinister.'

'It's obvious,' said Roderick, speaking with difficulty, 'that you've lost your standards.'

'According to your letter, I never had any. Do understand, Roderick, please, that Nicholas is very much in earnest and that the girl is in every way desirable and that they'll be married as soon as her father can overcome his prejudice against Nicholas.'

'Prejudice! Who in the devil's name does he think he is? Prejudice! A smuggler with prejudices!'

'Very deep ones. He's far more bitterly opposed to this marriage than you are.'

'Then he's got the glimmerings of a conscience, that's all I can say. I hope he'll manage to keep his daughter out of reach.'

'I wouldn't build on that, if I were you.'

'Did Martin tell you about his hare-brained hobby?'

'Yes. There's a woman staying with me who's trying to arrange business connections for him.'

'Anybody who thinks there's anything in that crack-brained rubbish is out of their minds. Good God! Can you imagine anybody in their senses going out and screwing imitation flowers into damn silly imitation stalks?'

'Yes,' said Lorna. 'I can.'

'You'll lead the boy on a wild-goose chase, and at the end of it he'll be nowhere. The idea's not only crazy, it's—it's disgusting. It's indecent. A garden is a garden, and you won't make a garden by sticking pseudo stems into the ground and fixing fake flowers on to them and calling it a garden. I'm surprised that even you can't see that. The boy's got to get down to

102

a real job and stick to it.'

'You must try to convince him.'

'With you working against me, I suppose?'

'I've told you they're not children any more. They'll do what they want to do.'

'All I'm afraid of is that they'll do what you encourage them to do. Well, I know where I stand, at all events. I'd just like to point out that I've had the care of them for the past eighteen years, and the results aren't bad.'

'Even you couldn't spoil them.'

'Thank you. I don't think we've anything more to say.'

'I don't think we have,' said Lorna.

'Then I'll get along. Perhaps you'll tell Martin that I'd like to see him in Gibraltar as soon as possible. I can get hold of Nicholas at any time, but Martin—'

'You can see Martin whenever you please, here or there,' said Lorna coldly. 'He has his own rooms and nobody will disturb you.'

'Thank you. Don't bother to come out. Good-bye.'

'Good-bye.'

He paused at the door and looked around. He would have liked to say something, but he was not clear what. He wished to compliment her on her looks, which he acknowledged to be far beyond the promise of her youth. He wanted to point out that the house made a perfect setting for her. He wanted to tell her that the sight of her, though it had roused in

103

him nothing but irritation, had in some way made him realize what they had both missed. Waste, waste, waste.

He wanted, most of all, to use her name. She had called him Roderick once at this meeting. He wanted to say Lorna—just once before he went away for ever. For memory's sake. Lorna. Lorna. But it would not come. He tried, but without success, and so he gave it up, and his face remained as hard and unmoved as it had done throughout their meeting, and he spoke with the same level finality.

'Good-bye,' he said.

CHAPTER EIGHT

Don Manrique and his wife lived on a large estate near the village of Yago, which nestled in the mountains about eight miles from the Casa del Carmen, at the end of a steep road whose surface was nothing less than appalling and which had done great damage to the already deplorable springs and tyres of Nicholas' car. The house was a rambling old Moorish one of rose-red stone; inside it all was cool and bare and quiet; outside it there were flowers and pigs and chickens and vines and goats and a stream in which the village women washed their clothes. It was very picturesque.

Nicholas sat on an uncomfortable cane chair

in one corner of the spacious patio of Don Manrique's house. Beside him on a smaller chair sat Carmela. Across the patio sat her father and mother. But Martin, who had come up to take their attention off his brother, was nowhere to be seen. He had discovered that Don Manrique's stables contained horses of outstanding beauty and breeding, and he had forgotten his reason for going up to Yago; all his attention was centred and all his time taken up in the contemplation of the splendid animals. Don Manrique rolled cigarettes and smoked them leisurely; his wife sat in calm repose. Where an Englishwoman would had her sewing, Señora Fernandez had her fan. From time to time she flicked it open with a practised deftness, fluttered it and closed it again.

Nicholas was counting his blessings. The evening had not been a great success, but was not over yet. The lateness of the Spanish dinner hour was, at the moment, his greatest source of contentment. They had not dined until almost ten, and now they sat in the cool dusk under the light of the stars; some additional illumination from the house shone on to Don Manrique and his wife and left Nicholas and Carmela in semi-obscurity. Nicholas had chosen the site with great forethought and now had his reward; if Carmela's father knew that his daughter's little hand was clasped in a large strong one he made no sign.

They sat for the most part in silence. Don Manrique had exhausted his English; Nicholas and Señora Fernandez had smiled at one another with a warmth that had dissolved the language difficulty. Now they sat silent, and Nicholas held Carmela's hand and looked round at the picturesqueness of his surroundings and mused on the Spanish way of life as he knew it from his mother's house and at this large, rambling mountain retreat.

There was abundance here, as there was down at the Casa del Carmen; profusion, even. But it was more evident here; the eye could see it and the nose could smell it. Fowls roosted on the trees outside the patio—Nicholas had known in a vague way that a hen was a bird, but he had never seen the fact demonstrated so clearly. On a slope behind the house he could see the dark shapes of goats being driven down the hillside in the care of a small boy. He listened to the chatter from the distant kitchen, and wondered whether an English hostess would have sat as placidly as Señora Fernandez while the unrestrained chatter and laughter of the maids sounded all round her. There seemed to be, here, service as ready as that at the Casa del Carmen, but down there the servants' friends and relations and hangers-on were not allowed within such close range. Like the livestock, they dwelt apart in small cottages out of sight and sound of the main building. Here they seemed to Nicholas to be an integral part of the family; goats and hens walked in and out unregarded; unidentified small girls in ragged dresses stood and stared, or sat in a circle near Don Manrique's chair. One of them rose, took the fan from the hand of Señora Fernandez, and fanned her tirelessly. Buxom young women passed to and fro, humming carelessly; one of them glanced down at her mistress' feet and, going into the house, returned with a pair of slippers. She stooped and, disregarding Señora Fernandez' murmur of protest, took away her high-heeled black shoes and helped her on with the more comfortable footwear, with a vigorous sentence which Nicholas took to be, 'Of course he won't mind; you know you always have your slippers on at this time.'

The housework went on in full view; tables were scrubbed, the tile floors were wiped clean; the house assumed the freshly polished appearance that contrasted so strongly with the less hygienic conditions out of doors. The servants left, one by one, to join their friends in the village and amuse themselves; in the morning they would reappear to cook on the primitive charcoal stoves, to scrub linen on the great stone sinks or on the rocky river banks, to milk goats and to make bread.

A murmur came from Señora Fernandez through the dusk, and Nicholas heard Carmela reply. Then her mother gave the curious brief, hissing sound that seemed to be the local

107

equivalent of pressing a bell; a smiling maid appeared, scurried away and came back with a wrap for her young mistress. Obviously Carmela's mother had felt that some protection was necessary against the night air. The wrap was of black lace, as delicate as a spider's web; Carmela draped it carelessly over her head and Nicholas, looking at her delicate face, her enormous eyes peeping from beneath the lace folds, found himself suddenly upon his feet and walking to and fro with Carmela's little hand tucked firmly under his arm. He looked at the wooded patch outside the patio, and measured the distance with a trained eye: if he could add two yards to the limit of his pacing, and then another two yards ...

They were not out of sight, but one tree had a trunk of useful width; it could screen two people if they were close enough together. It was not wise to linger there too long, for Don Manrique's chair had creaked ominously the last time. Indiscretion could bring disaster: the night air would be pronounced too much for Carmela, and they would all go inside and sit in the large, bare, tiled hall, in soft but baffling lamp-light.

Nicholas, from the shade of the wood, looked across at Don Manrique and saw his brows drawn together in a frown of deep displeasure. He was somewhat surprised, for although he was aware that his suit found no favour, Don Manrique had always shown a

108

grave courtesy that masked whatever he might be thinking of his guest. Nicholas tried to put himself in Don Manrique's place and to see the matter from his point of view, but he had done so many times before and had come back each time to the same conclusion: that although he was not fit to lick Carmela's little shoes, he could give her almost as much as any other man who dared to lift his eyes to her. He could bring her a whole heart, a strong body and a position as a Naval officer's wife that even the Queen of England hadn't scorned. He wished that he had Spanish enough to point this out to Don Manrique. If the old fellow, he thought yearningly, if the old fellow would only look at the thing reasonably. And he would, too, if he had any idea of the warmth, the depth, the fire of his daughter's passions. Nicholas, with a protective clasp of the hand within his own, remembered the touchingly sweet manner of her surrender. She had been, at first, trembling and shy. She had loved him, but she had kept him at arm's length. And then, one day, she had come into his arms and lifted her lips to his and ... Nicholas, remembering his own gentleness, his astounding self-command, his resolute unclasping of the warm arms from round his neck, his misty, groping determination to protect her, to protect them both until he could claim her openly, was staggered by its improbability. If anybody had told him that he could resist temptation in such

109

a form, he would have strenuously denied it.

It was some time before Don Manrique broke under the strain and swept them all indoors. Nicholas felt that the interludes behind the tree had been tantalizingly brief, but they had been better than nothing. Much, much better. He could still feel her sweetness on his lips, and as he drove away with Martin down the steep, rutted road, he was uplifted to the point of pouring out his feelings in poetry. He had never cared for poetry, but on a night like this, with the moon beginning to illuminate the expanse of sea far below, with the lights of Estronella twinkling at his feet, with the pale outline of the wall round the Casa del Carmen drawing a chalk-mark beside the coast road, this, this was the time for poetry. The heart could not speak in prose; it must spill over in lovely stanzas.

'Carmela,' began Nicholas, spilling over,

'Carmela, my lovely Carmela,
Oh, come to the arms of your sailor—'

'That's not supposed to be p-poetic, is it?' enquired Martin.

'Can you do any better?'

'I couldn't do much worse. How would you like,

Oh moon! your beams grow faint, grow paler

In the light that gleams in the eyes of my Carmela?'

'That's got no metre,' objected Nicholas.

'No, but it's got more depth and more, as it were, meaning. One would work on it, one could play with that second line and make more of it—no, less of it.'

* * *

It was late when Nicholas and Martin reached the Casa del Carmen, but Lorna was waiting for them in her sitting-room, and coffee and sandwiches were ordered, and a bed prepared for Nicholas if he should decide to stay. She listened to their account of the visit to Yago before she broke her own news; when she at last told them, her tone was so casual that it was difficult for them to grasp the sense of what she had said.

'Father—here?' said Martin.

'Good Lord!' said Nicholas.

'He must have moved f-fast,' commented Martin. 'Mother, what did it feel like to see him after all this time?'

'Did he bully you?' asked Nicholas.

'Nobody can bully me,' said Lorna calmly. 'He merely stated his objections to whatever you and Martin were doing, and I told him to take them to the proper quarter.'

'Oh, Mother!' said Nicholas. 'Didn't you

talk about Carmela? Didn't you tell him he's got to see her? Didn't he sound at all reasonable?'

'I don't think we dwelt on Carmela,' said Lorna. 'We discussed Don Manrique.'

'*Mother!*' Nicholas pushed his hands through his hair and left it standing up stiffly. 'Mother, didn't you fix a meeting between him and Carmela? Didn't you tell him—'

'I told him that it was nothing to do with me.'

'But good Lord! You're the one person who can do anything! You *promised*, Mother darling! When are you seeing Father again?'

'Never, I hope,' said Lorna.

This calm rejoinder brought the eyes of both her sons on her in a long, level stare. Lorna looked back at them with as much confidence as she could muster, but a shade of uncertainty took the edge from her next words.

'Let me make something clear,' she said. 'I can't and I won't interfere between you and your father. I don't say that I won't do all I can to help you both, but you must see him and talk to him and work out your own affairs with him. I'll do all I can to talk Don Manrique round and make him agree to Carmela's marrying you, Nicholas, and I'll back Florence if she thinks of anything reasonable for Martin. But I'm not—I am not going to engage in a growling match with your father, with you two boys as the bones. He and I have different outlooks, and we don't agree about this, or about anything. We're working for different results, and so the less we meet the happier it'll be for us all. This is my home and I'm very happy in it, and I'll welcome you both whenever you care to come and stay here. But do keep your father out of my way, that's all I ask.'

Nobody answered this long and reasoned speech. Nicholas and Martin looked at one another, and their glance summed up everything they felt about parents, about mothers, about women and women's unreasonableness. They sighed gently, patiently. Martin came to sit beside Lorna on the sofa, and Nicholas perched on the arm. Their voices were full of forbearance.

'look, Mother darling—' began Nicholas.

'My p-pet,' said Martin.

'Try to see it this way,' said Nicholas, his arm affectionately about her shoulders. 'The old man's here; he's arrived breathing fire and so on, and he'll do everything he can to make us see what he calls reason.'

'He won't talk,' said Martin. 'He's a man of action, Mama.'

'He'll act and soon,' said Nicholas. 'He's got untold pull in the right quarters. He'll have me transferred by next week, and I'll be half-way to Iceland before I know what's happened.'

'He'll have my f-flowers confiscated as some kind of contraband,' said Martin. 'He won't just sit there in Gib, you know, Mother. He'll get busy, and he'll make an awful lot of t-trouble.'

'Everything,' said Nicholas, in the tone of a teacher coaxing a backward pupil, 'everything hangs on you. Father's here and two things can happen: he can be left to himself in Gib, doing untold harm and wrecking everything, or he can—'

'This house is really a p-perfect headquarters,' pointed out Martin.

'Mother'—Nicholas spoke urgently—'you've got to have him here now and again. Left to himself he'll sit down and think it all out like a chief of staff planning combined ops, and then he'll bite his way through all our plans. You don't have to be friendly about this; you merely invite him out here to parley, and while he's parleying, we can go on with our plans without fear of their getting chewed up and ruined. All we need is a little more time.'

'A little time and a little c-co-operation from you,' said Martin. 'That's all, darling.'

'That's all,' said Nicholas. 'Father'll be dangerous if you leave him there with the opportunity of tying everything up into knots. You've got to get him out here and keep him busy driving out here and back, and talking it all over and—'

'P-parleying,' said Martin.

'You know quite well,' said Lorna, 'that your father isn't a fool. This is nothing but

114

childish foolishness. He'll know perfectly well that—'

'Of course he will,' said Nicholas. 'But Martin's right, this house is what he said, the perfect headquarters. That's all we want. We need to form a united front. We need—cohesion. If father's left to float about in Gib, if Martin's got to go to and fro interviewing him, if I'm to have him hanging round my tail, if you're to sit out here in splendid isolation, then nothing can come right. It's too untidy, for one thing. But if you'll let us close up a bit—look, Mother, I'll get a few days leave, and I'll come out and stay here. That makes us a trio, you and Martin and myself. All you've got to do is to tell Father that, after thinking things over, you feel that you and he must both—just for the moment—sink your differences. Put out a hand, and as he's not a churl, what can he do but grasp it?'

'What can be a more perfect headquarters?' asked Martin. 'This place has got atmosphere—a nice, peaceful, d-disarming atmosphere. That routs the enemy, for a start. And then there's the other angle—the guest-under-your-roof angle. He can't really let himself go here.'

'It's one thing for him to get hold of influential ears and behave like an outraged father and get me sent into Arctic waters to cool off,' said Nicholas. 'But it's quite another thing to appear as an ex-husband, a frequent guest in your house, with your sons—and his—seated between you both. It makes his case look a good deal less convincing, doesn't it?'

'D-decidedly weak,' said Martin. 'T-tottery, in fact.'

'Mother darling,' begged Nicholas, 'will you let us manage this?'

'I entirely disagree,' said Lorna, 'with any—'

'Mama,' said Nicholas, 'you can't sit on the fence. You've got to be either for us or against us.'

'Don't be silly, Nicholas,' she said. 'You know perfectly well that I'll do anything I can—within reason. But—'

'Hush!' said Nicholas. 'Don't spoil it.'

'You're s-sweet,' said Martin. 'I'm going to name a flower after you. I'll call it Lupin Lorna Salvador. It'll be lovely.'

'Everything,' prophesied Nicholas, 'is going to be lovely.'

'Good,' said Lorna, drily. 'Now will you finish up the sandwiches and go to bed.'

CHAPTER NINE

Florence never rose before breakfast and was seldom seen before lunch, but on the following day at noon, she sent a servant down to her brother's caravan to inform him that she wished to see him.

Woolly walked up obediently, and Florence saw that she had not been mistaken in thinking that his behaviour on the previous evening had been almost normal. She had dined out, and on her return she had walked down to see her brother and had found, to her relief, that he was able to converse with a greater degree of clarity than at any time since his arrival at the Casa del Carmen. There was not much to choose between the Woolly bemused by Lorna's beauty and the one in what Florence chose to call his right mind, but he was now in a state in which he could understand what was said to him, and she was impatient to see Martin in a flourishing business—the kind of business was not clear, but the profits would pour in; Martin would be rich and his father would be biting his nails with chagrin at not having bought up the bulk of the shares.

Of Roderick's arrival and visit to the house, she had as yet no idea; she had not seen Lorna since lunch on the previous day, and although she knew that Nicholas had stayed the night, she didn't know whether or not he had returned to Gibraltar yet. He hadn't. Her sense of urgency was merely the result of her having had to wait, doing nothing, while her brother sat outside his waggon dreaming of Lorna.

She greeted him briefly when he entered, and then went straight to the point.

'Look, Woolly,' she said, 'I've been very patient. I asked you to come here and you

117

came, and I'm glad, but what have you done since you've been here?'

'Well, let me see, Flo,' began Woolly, who had never heard of a rhetorical question. 'I—'

'I'll tell you what you've done,' said Florence. 'You've done nothing.'

'But see here, Flo, I only got here—'

'It doesn't matter when you got here, Woolly. That's neither here nor there. I told them you were a businessman, and that as soon as you saw Martin's flowers, you'd think up a scheme to turn them into good money. And what did you do?'

'I told you. I like those flowers, Flo, but I haven't got round to thinking what to do.'

'You've just been walking round like a man struck by lightning.'

'In a manner of speaking, Flo, I was—'

'Struck by lightning. Yes, she's beautiful, but you ought to know that if you wanted to please her, the thing to do would have been to do something for her son. That's sense, isn't it? Woolly, I'm your only sister, and you've got to help me.'

Woolly looked a little dazed. Florence had been his sister for more than half a century, and had never applied to him for help before.

'I'll help you, Flo, and glad to. But what did you have in mind?'

Florence hesitated. She had had nothing in mind but doing something to prove to everybody concerned that Martin's preoccupation with artificial gardens could be turned to useful, to profitable account. But Woolly had an irritating way of requiring problems to be set out in the plainest possible terms, and then he had his own method of dealing with them.

Woolly's detractors had more than once referred to his brain as a sieve, and the term, offered in no spirit of compliment, was in fact an accurate one. Other people's ideas and opinions were received by him with guarded suspicion and subjected to a long process of filtering. He had a simple and ineradicable belief that most people talked nonsense, and he considered it essential that a man should have some system by which he could separate the wheat of wisdom from the conversational chaff. Woolly sieved, or perhaps he dredged; whatever the process, it was necessarily a lengthy one, and at the end of it, Woolly had rejected everything but what he felt to be the germ of common sense.

'I hadn't got it worked out,' she said at last. 'All it seemed to me was that there was money there, if only somebody would think out a way of making it. Those flowers ought to be on the market. You're a man, can't you do something?'

'Well, Flo, I haven't done much thinking about it. But if you want me to, I'll go out there and look for Martin and talk to him.'

'You won't have to look for him. I've sent

119

him a message to say you'd like to see him. So you've got to say something, Woolly, and you've got to say it as though you meant it. I told them, may the Lord forgive me, that you were a businessman.'

'I am a businessman, Flo,' pointed out Woolly mildly.

'You trade; that's not what I meant. I meant one of those you read about, the ones who spin a dime and it comes down a dollar. I wanted you to come here and impress everybody.'

'I don't think I could impress anybody, Flo.'

'Well, we won't argue about it. Tell me honestly, Woolly, what did you think of Martin's flowers?'

'Those flowers of his?'

'Yes.'

'Those flowers he gets up to look like real ones?'

'Yes. What do you think of them?'

Woolly took some time to consider.

'I think,' he said at last, 'that they look like real ones.'

There was a pause. Florence picked up a heavy ornament from a table beside her, fingered it longingly, and put it down again.

'Woolly,' she said, in a voice she strove to keep low and gentle, 'do you think anybody would ever buy them?'

'Buy them, Flo?'

'If *you* wanted a garden, Woolly, and if you were sick and couldn't get out to work at one,

120

wouldn't you like to look out from your bed where you're lying and see a nice garden all ready made?'

'Yes, Flo. I think perhaps I might.'

'Then look, Woolly; remember that you'd like it yourself, and go out there and talk to Martin about it. Think up some way you'd be able to go out and buy a ready-made garden whenever you felt like it. Think how you'd—' Exhaustion overcame her, and she leaned back and waved a hand weakly toward the door. 'Just go on, Woolly, and talk to him.'

He went out and joined Martin on the terrace, and they sat on long, comfortable chairs and looked at one another across a low table and a tray of iced drinks. No setting could have been more conducive to pleasant discussion, but Woolly appeared to be ill at ease.

'Is it too cool for you out here,' enquired Martin, seeing his restiveness.

'Oh no. No. I wouldn't say it was too cool.'

'Do you find it too warm?'

'Warm? Oh no. No. I wouldn't say it was too warm.'

'Would you like to go somewhere else?'

Martin's voice was patient, soothing and friendly. This was not his idea of a forceful personality, but he was willing to believe Florence's statement that all her brother's brain was absorbed by his business deals. To Martin he looked like the problem child in a

121

kindergarten: gentle, eager, ready to take it all in, if the teacher could get it in.

'Where would you like to go?' he asked.

'Now, that's a good idea,' said Woolly, with relief. 'It's just as you say, of course, but it's kind of formal up here, and at any minute Flo might jump out and say—that is, she—'

'Women like interrupting,' said Martin. 'Where d'you think we'll be s-safe from them?'

'Well, now. Down at my place?' pleaded Woolly. 'It's quiet, and it's comfortable, too.'

Martin went with frank pleasure. He had been to Woolly's waggon several times, but there was always more to be seen. It's surprises were inexhaustible. They walked through the garden and came to the large, incongruous, canvas-covered vehicle that had now sprouted off-shoots which had little resemblance to the parent body. Woolly led the way to a small, open tent and unfolded two chairs.

'We'll set down here,' he said. 'I like this view of the sea.'

'It's peaceful,' said Martin.

'Yes, it's peaceful, son, and that's how I like it. I can't seem to do much thinking when there's a lot of schuffle round me. I like to get on my own and take my time.'

He took his time and Martin, examining some unfamiliar aspects of the chair in which he sat, discovered that it was Woolly-made, and had a leg rest and adjustable arms and a device that made it rock, or not rock,

122

according to taste. Martin rocked and fell into a light doze, and woke up and found that Woolly had begun to say something.

'These flowers of yours,' he said. 'Flo thinks you could sell them, son.'

'I know she does. She's very kind,' said Martin, 'but I think I ought to tell you f-frankly, at once, that I don't agree with her—that is, I don't think they'd ever sell on a large scale. I say, this neckrest's pretty clever. I've only just noticed it.'

'If you want to set,' said Woolly, 'then you want to set comfortable. That's why I put in those improvements. What did you have in mind, son?'

'Me? Oh, you mean about my f-flowers?'

'That's so.'

'Well, nothing commercial, at least not in any big way. I—crumbs!'

'Now, now son, that screw makes it fold up, see? You didn't want to touch that one. Did you hurt yourself?'

'I enj-joyed it. You could have some fun with that.'

'I didn't know you'd go touching those screws. There now, I've got it fixed up.'

'T-thanks. What was I in the middle of saying? Oh, yes. No, I just thought I might find a place where I could put the things on view somewhere and find out what people thought of them.'

'But suppose they wanted to buy them, son?

What would you do then?'

'Well, I hadn't ever got as far as that.'

'But it seems to me that if people want them, you'll have to have some to sell them.'

'I s-suppose so.'

'And that means that you'll have to produce them,' said Woolly, following this clear trail.

'Yes.'

'And then, if you went in for making them in a big way, you'd want a lot of people to know about them, wouldn't you?'

'Probably.'

'And before people could get to know about them, you'd have to find some way to tell them.'

'Very likely.'

'It's no use producing something that people don't know anything about. That's sweet reason, isn't it, son?'

'Yes.'

'Then as I see it,' said Woolly, with growing confidence, 'the first thing to do would be to advertise it.'

'Advertise?'

'Yes, son. I could see about it when I got back home.'

'Back home? You mean in Canada?'

'That's where I come from.'

'Yes, I know, but I rather imagined—I don't know why—that you lived in this—this c-caravan all the time, sort of wandering about.'

'I do, and then again, I don't,' explained

Woolly. 'But I'm going back in a month or so, and I could take this idea back with me and work on it.'

'But all I thought of was just a—well, an old English cottage garden.'

'They go for English cottages over there,' said Woolly. 'They run them up all over the place. When I was a boy, I did a spell with a builder's outfit, and we put up just whatever the customer asked for. You can put up a house in no time, but the gardens—now you come to think of it, son, you don't get gardens so easy. And if this idea of yours could give the customers a garden at the same time you gave 'em a house, why then, I'll tell you this: it isn't a bad idea. There's sense to it. A lot of good sense. A house with a garden. But it seems to me that flowers by themselves wouldn't make a garden. You'd have to have more than that. You'd have to have all the other things that people want in their gardens. You'd have to have crazy paths. I don't see why I couldn't work up a little idea for crazy paths. Folks could buy 'em in strips, like a carpet, and roll 'em out. And they'd want rockeries. Well, I could get an idea for a rockery. I've got an idea for rocks—you could make 'em light as a feather and like rocks, so like rocks, son, that you wouldn't know the difference, not till you picked one up to throw at the fellow next door. And grass. Grass. No, I don't have an idea for grass.'

125

'All I wanted,' said Martin, 'was to—'

'This thing,' said Woolly, entirely carried away, 'is a follow-on from all the things they've thought up to make things easy for the housewife. Over there in Canada a young woman starts up house, and see what's she's got: she's got herself ready-to-mix cakes; she's got minute rice and minute tapioca and ready-cooked meats, and meals that you take out of the freezer and put straight in front of a man at the table. Does she go out and dig herself up vegetables and wash 'em and peel 'em? No, son. Why, no. She buys 'em all ready frozen in a see-through packet, and all she's got to do is unwrap 'em and drop 'em into the hot water. Inside her house she's got machines to wash her clothes and machines to wash her dishes. She's doing fine indoors. But now you come out front with me and take a look at that plot. Come out back and take a look at her yard. Why, son—' Woolly gave a gesture eloquent of hopelessness and slumped down despairingly in his chair—'it's a mess! They haven't had the house long, see, and they've had their hands full, fixing things inside the house. The garden just went plumb to hell. And that's where I come in. I drive up in a truck—no, first I send in a bulldozer to level it out. Then I send the truck in. I'll have 'em painted a nice fancy colour, with flowers. The customer chooses what he wants in his garden, just as he chooses his furniture or his wallpaper or the colour of his

126

paint. I send in the men, and they put in the flowers, lay the crazy paving and fix up any extras like a rockery or a lavender hedge or a pergola like that one over there or some fancy arches with roses on 'em. They—'

Woolly's words came to an abrupt stop and his long, gangling figure came slowly upright in his chair. Martin, looking at him in astonishment, saw that he was listening intently.

'What—' he began.

'Sh!,' said Woolly, one hand upraised. 'Can you hear that?'

Martin could hear a great deal: the surge of the sea, the wind in the branches, the distant cries of children or the voices of fishermen farther along the shore. But Woolly had risen and, going into the largest of the tents, had come out again carrying a little reed pipe, and on this he began to play, haltingly, a plaintive little air. It seemed to be an echo, and then Martin realized that Woolly was, in fact, echoing the sounds that came from somewhere far along the beach—a plaintive, haunting melody that seemed to have no beginning and no end, that trilled and trembled and ended at last on a long, expectant note.

Woolly took the pipe from his lips.

'I didn't get that,' he said.

'That tune? Why d'you want to,' enquired Martin.

'That's a kind of hobby of mine, son,' said

127

Woolly. 'Wherever I go, I take this little fellow with me and play tunes that belong to the places I'm in.'

'Do you write them down?'

'Me? No, I don't write them down, son. I play 'em over and over and over, and I get them in my head and take 'em home with me, tunes that I hear in little out-of-the-way places, all kinds. I learn them, and then when I get back home, I play 'em over to the boys until they know them, and when they do, by golly, they make 'em sound fine.'

'What boys?'

'My boys. The boys who work for me back home. I've got a fine bunch of boys. The best. They've been with me—most of them—longer than they can count.'

'What do you—they do?'

'Do? I buy horses and sell horses,' said Woolly.

'Horses!' Martin's eyes widened with surprise. 'I—I love horses.'

'You do? Then you must come over and see mine. If we're going to get together and put gardens on the market—Horses and gardens. They don't seem to go together, somehow.'

'But I thought that you—well, you've got this travelling house and—'

'Why yes, son. But that doesn't mean I'm travelling for nothing but pleasure. I'm here to buy horses. I buy 'em everywhere, but if you want the best, you have to come to where they keep the best. I don't know much about anything—except horses. I've had a Derby winner, once.'

'A—you mean the English Derby?'

'That's just what I mean. I sold a horse to a man who sold it to a man who brought it over from Canada and won a Derby with it. Flo says I'm not much good at figures, but even Flo admits that I know a good horse when I see one. But in between buying I get a lot of time to put in the best way I can, and at night, lying down and waiting to go to sleep, I used to hear tunes. I can pick up a tune if I hear it two or three times, but round these parts, they don't play tunes you can pin down. They're mostly these—'

'Moorish?'

'Suppose so. You hear a girl singing round here, and it doesn't sound like any tune out of the West. Always brings up Eastern bazaars to my mind. Like that little tune awhile back.'

There was a peaceful silence. Martin had long since discarded his chair and was lying on the grass near-by, his arms linked behind his head, his eyes sometimes on Woolly, sometimes on the foliage waving far above his head. He felt at peace and at home. His liking for the tall, bald, simple-minded, simple-hearted man beside him was increasing steadily. This was not the ordinary conception of the keen businessman, but Martin felt, nevertheless, that any scheme would be safe in

Woolly's long, thin hands. He had seemed to come round the subject from a long way off; he had circled round it, but he seemed, now, to have adopted it and made it his own.

'Tell me,' asked Woolly, after a long, restful interval, 'how long you been working on those flowers of yours, son?'

Martin counted.

'Twelve years or more, I suppose,' he said at last. 'I think I s-started when I was about nine or ten, and I've been at it, more or less, ever since then.'

'With me, it was horses,' said Woolly. 'My folks had a hard time fixing me up. They tried to make me into a builder; then they tried something else. And then something else. But I saved up and bought a horse. It didn't look much, but there was something about it. That was the first horse that ever I was on, and he taught me more than I taught him. And I sold him for a lot more than I gave for him and surprised everybody except myself. A fellow knows—'

'Wheeee!' A long, low whistle had come from Martin, and Woolly saw that he was standing up and staring through the trees.

'What's the matter, son?' he enquired.

'Horses!' said Martin.

'Yes, that's what I was telling you. I—'

'No, horses, here,' said Martin. 'Visitors. Don Manrique, b-by Jove! Woolly, now there are horses for you. Come and look.'

130

The visitors were Don Manrique and his daughter.

There had been a family parley in the patio of the house at Yago, and the subject of Nicholas, in his new guise, came up for discussion. Carmela said nothing; she looked through the open doorway of the patio to the profusion of camellias and jonquils blooming outside. She was small, not more than five feet, with soft black hair, a delicate skin and enormous dark eyes. She sat with her hands folded on her lap and thought about Nicholas. Her mother was also silent and seemed to be counting the glazed tiles that made a border of gay colour round the walls of the patio; she, too, was thinking of Nicholas, for whom she had a deep and romantic regard, the direct result of Nicholas' simple conviction that one way of winning the daughter was to go to work on the mother. Success had attended the scheme; she was entirely on his side, but she knew her husband's wishes and hesitated at the thought of giving Carmela too much encouragement. That was a young nice man, but this was a good husband.

Don Manrique, tiring of talking to himself, looked at his abstracted wife and daughter and realized that he was wasting his time. He rose, and with great good sense ordered the horses—he had an expensive car, but the mule tracks were better than the road—and went down to call upon Lorna.

131

He took his daughter with him, and Florence van Leyte saw them from her window as they rode up to the Casa del Carmen. She was in her sitting-room, trying to write letters and not succeeding very well because, from the desk at which she sat, she had a very good view of the garden, where a man on a donkey was collecting twigs and taking them away and coming back for more. The man was picturesque enough, in his large and sensible straw hat, but the donkey was enchanting, and Florence loved a donkey above all things. This one was small and pearly-grey, and his harness was a brilliant scarlet and he wore a blue tassel on his forehead and tossed it contemptuously whenever his owner suggested hurrying. Beyond the donkey was a tree which Florence could not name, but whose branches were laden with scarlet blossom; between the donkey and her window were flowers which she meant one day to identify, and which ranged in colour from the palest blue to the deepest purple. She wished she had a paint brush in her hand instead of a pen; she would not have been able to use it, but it would have looked more fitting.

At the sight of the two horses and their riders, Florence put down her pen and gave herself up to staring. She took in the grave dignity of Don Manrique on what looked to her like a charger, and then tore her eyes away to study the little Carmela, shy but composed

132

beneath her picturesque wide hat. Never, Florence told herself, in the whole of her life had she seen an outfit that achieved so perfect a balance between the purely functional and the entirely fancy. She rose impulsively and went searching through the house until she came upon Lorna in the large, stone-floored kitchen.

'Callers,' she announced. 'Lorna, you won't take them away into your sitting room and hide them, will you?'

Lorna gave some final directions in Spanish and followed her guest out of the kitchen.

'Who?' she asked.

'Nicholas' Spanish sweetie—and her father. I guess it's a business call, but they look so beautiful that I'd like to see more of them. If I go into the drawing-room and look as though I've been in there all the morning, will you promise to bring them in there?'

Lorna considered the question for a moment.

'Yes,' she said finally. 'Yes, I will. He'll want to see me alone, but I don't suppose anything could keep Nick away either.'

'Don't try to get me out of the room while they're here, Lorna, because I won't take any hint less plain than a prod in the rear. Be nice, now.'

'You'd better stay,' Lorna said thoughtfully. 'At this stage I don't think it would be wise to—'

'Quite right. It's too early for a show-down.

133

All you have to do now is to show that in future he's dealing with you and not with Nicholas.'

It was obvious that Don Manrique saw this clearly. He greeted Lorna, bowed gravely to Florence, refused refreshment and accepted a straight-backed chair. Carmela kissed her hostess, slid her hat back so that its strings supported it on her shoulders, and sank into a graceful little heap on a rug at Lorna's feet, only to find herself drawn up again gently by Nicholas, who came into the room and, after pausing only to greet her father, led Carmela outside into the sunshine. Hand in hand, they strolled down to the sea and sat on a low bench; Carmela talked and Nicholas listened, or half-listened, watching her lips and dreaming.

'You are not listening to me,' said Carmela, at last.

'Yes, I am. What were you saying?'

'About my aunt.'

'That was it; go on.'

'She is very sad,' said Carmela, in her soft voice. 'It is about her money.'

'That's a universal worry,' said Nicholas. 'Has she lost it or something?'

'Not exactly,' said Carmela, in her careful English. 'But it was all because of the bandits.'

'Bandits?'

'Yes. There are some bandits here, you know.'

'Well, I'd heard strong rumours, but I thought that it was almost too much to

134

believe.'

'Oh, yes, there are bandits. But they are not bad bandits, you understand?'

'I understand. They're good bandits, but they took her money, is that it?'

'No,' said Carmela. 'They wrote to her husband and asked him for money. It was a very polite letter.'

'I get them frequently. What did they want money for?'

'They did not say for what. They said that they needed the money, and that her husband was rich and had much to give. They told him, in the letter, how much they wanted, and they asked him to bring it to them at a certain place. They said that they would receive him with much courtesy. But they said that it would be better if he did not mention the letter to anybody; they said that as he was a gentleman and they were also gentlemen, he must treat the matter confidentially. If he did not, it might happen that bad thing would come to him.'

'This year of grace,' commented Nicholas. 'Well, he paid up, I suppose, and his wife's feeling a bit out of pocket?'

'No, he did not pay. He took the letter and he went with it to the police.'

'Good for him. And so the bad thing came to him and his widow's weeping?'

'No. You go too fast.'

'Sorry, darling. Kiss me. Now go on. He took the letter and he went with it to the police.'

'Yes. So they all went to the place where the bandits said they would be waiting for the money, but there was nobody there.'

'I hope they promoted the look-out man.'

'So they found no bandits, but the police said that as he had told them about the letter, it would be safer for him to have police protection. And so they sent six Guardias Civiles to his house.'

'Well, go on. That can't be the end.'

'Yes, that is all.'

'But what's she crying for?'

'The police have been in her house for six months, and she has had to feed them. She has spent more money on food for them than the bandits asked for in the first place. And so she has come to ask my father to make the police go away. When her husband asks them, they say that he still needs protection.'

They sat in silent commiseration, and Nicholas listened to sounds which he knew he would remember all his life, but which he felt he would not, once, have associated with romance. The birds sang, if hens could be said to be birds, and if they could sing; there were scents, but they came from the goats grazing on a patch of grass somewhere behind them. There was soft breathing, but it came from a pig which had broken its tether and was enjoying a brief and unaccustomed freedom. The song of spring was supplied by a donkey who, on passing a friend less laden then himself, gave voice to long and loud indignation. Technically, mused Nicholas, listening to the raucous braying, none of it made for the ideal background of courtship, but these were smells and sounds, nevertheless, which he had listened to in Carmela's mountain home and which he had come to associate with sweet and delirious moments.

He looked down at the dark head nestling against his arm, and Carmela, glancing up, sensed his change of mood and came closer.

'Nicholas,' she said.

'Yes?'

'Everything is going so slowly. The days go by, and soon you will have to go away, but nothing is settled.'

'It's slow work,' admitted Nicholas. 'But darling, I'm doing my best.'

'I have told my mother that we must marry. I have said that I will marry nobody but you, but she says that if I tell my father that my mind is made up, he will send me away.'

'I'm quite sure he will. I honestly can't see, Carmela, what he's got against me.'

'I can see—a little. I am his only child, and it will mean that I shall go far away from him.'

'If he wants to see you,' pointed out Nicholas, 'all he's got to do is hop on a plane, and he'll be in England in a few hours.'

'You are sure you would not like to have a house here?'

'Quite sure, darling. We'll come here on

visits, but we've got to have a home in England. Can you bear that?'

'Quite easily. Do you like me to kiss you softly, like that?'

'Yes, but let's talk business first, my sweet.'

Carmela looked at him, her dark eyes thoughtful. She was making a great many adjustments, and she was making them, on the whole, without assistance. Her life had been, hitherto, pleasant and uncomplicated; she had been happy and petted—pampered, perhaps, for she had never in her life had to do anything for herself. But she was surprisingly unspoilt, and she was also blessed with a mixture of her mother's placidity and her father's common sense. The touch of arrogance that characterized many girls of her class and nationality was softened, in Carmela, by a natural laziness. She had had nothing to do but pass the time as pleasantly as possible; there had not even been the need to plan the future, for the future was sure to arrange itself; she was pretty and popular, and it only remained to choose this one or that one.

Nicholas had entirely shattered this tranquil existence. She had set out one morning for a ride, leaving a home in which everything was going on as usual. Four hours later she had come back again, but things had changed, and they were never to be the same again. An Englishman, tall, impetuous, persistent, determined and completely oblivious of the increasing coolness of his welcome had sprung, uninvited, on to the family coach and appeared to have no intention of leaving it until one of its members disembarked with him. He was handsome, but Carmela had seen many handsome men; she had liked him, but she had liked others as much, and yet this time it seemed to be different. Something had changed, and she woke up one morning to realize the full extent of the change.

Knowing herself, at last, in love, she discovered that for the first time in her life she had to think for herself. For the first time her mother's calmness brought no ease and her father's opinions found no echo in her own mind. For the first time she was alone and facing a future very different from the one she had grown up to expect.

She had hesitated for a while before confessing to Nicholas that she loved him. When she told him, she told him sweetly and without reservation. To his passionate pleading, she at last gave a passionate response, only to find that after the first heady embraces, Nicholas had turned without warning from a warm-blooded youth into a cool-headed man. It was extremely puzzling; he had besought her to come into his arms and she had come, and he was now behaving like a man who, having disposed of one problem, was ready to go on to the next. It was no longer, 'Carmela, Carmela I love you so'; it was, 'Let's

139

talk business first, my sweet.' This, perhaps, was the English courtship.

'I'm listening, Nicholas,' she said.

'You'll be lonely in England when I have to go away and you can't come with me.'

'There will be all our children.'

'After a bit, yes.'

'They will be half Spanish.'

'Yes, I suppose they will,' admitted Nicholas with a shade of reluctance.

'Will your father come to see us when we are married?'

'Of course.' Nicholas hesitated. 'He—he's here, Carmela.'

'Here?'

'Not in this house, no. He's in Spain, that is, he's at Gibraltar.'

Carmela considered this piece of news, but to Nicholas, watching her anxiously, it did not seem that she was unduly disquieted. Nor was she; for Carmela the chief stumbling block in the path of their courtship was not Nicholas' father but her own. She crept into Nicholas' arms, and he put her firmly away from him.

'Why are you so unfriendly?' she asked.

'Because, Carmela, one of us has got to do the thinking. And one of us has got to keep an eye on the temperature, too. Take your arms away—there, now. The other one, too. And sit farther away. That's it.'

'You don't love me?'

'For the moment it's safer to assume that I

don't. Now listen, I'm going to talk to my father. I'm going to tell him that we've made up our minds and that we're going to be married as soon as possible.'

'Oh, Nicholas—'

'Stay where you are. Then I'll ask my mother to help me to go ahead with all the arrangements, just as though we'd got the blessing of all concerned. If we wait any longer, it'll be too late; I'll be away and—well, it'll be too late, anyway.'

'Is that all you are going to say?'

'That's all.'

'Can I come back again.'

'Yes, you can come back.'

The approach of a servant, some minutes later, told them they were summoned, and they rose to return to the house.

The visit had not, from Don Manrique's point of view, been a success. He had come eight miles, all of them downhill and difficult riding, to assess Lorna's reactions to the new situation. She would, he realized, be on her son's side, but she was not wholly English; she had good Spanish blood in her veins and she understood deeply and thoroughly the Spanish traditions and way of life—something that no foreigner, and particularly no Englishman, could understand. She was his friend; she would know his wishes. He had come to see her, but now he understood, from Florence's continued presence in the room, that Lorna

141

was not ready to exchange views. He sighed, spoke for a time on trivial matters and then at the return of his daughter and Nicholas rose and bowed his farewells. The horses were brought round, not by their regular grooms, but by Martin and Woolly, and Don Manrique enjoyed for a short while a conversation which was confined entirely to horseflesh and which gave him the only pleasure he got from the visit. His opinion of Martin, already high, rose greatly, and in Woolly he recognized a man who knew all there was to know about a good horse. He went away with spirits somewhat lightened; Nicholas and Martin accompanied the cavalcade to the outer gate, and Lorna was left with Florence and Woolly on the porch.

'That man,' said Florence, staring after Don Manrique thoughtfully, 'reminds me of something out of a play. He does everything in slow motion, like a king in full regalia. Lorna, do all those rumours about him mean anything?'

'What rumours?' asked Woolly.

'They say he's the chippiest smuggler in these parts,' Florence told him. 'Lorna, is it true?'

Lorna smiled.

'I don't know,' she said.

'Smuggler?' said Woolly, in surprise.

'He's a very rich man, isn't he?' asked Florence.

'Yes, I think he is,' said Lorna.

'He comes of a good family,' said Florence thoughtfully. 'He could own it all legitimately, couldn't he?'

'He could,' said Lorna, 'but when he came here, he was relatively poor.'

'I see. And now he's got money, and there's nothing to show where it came from, is that it?' went on Florence.

'Something like that.' said Lorna.

'He's got some fine horses,' said Woolly. 'You mean he's supposed to be some kind of smuggler?'

'But smuggling is an honourable profession—almost,' said Lorna.

'You know and I know. But if it's so honourable, why don't those Guardias Civiles know too? Why do they go after the smugglers every so often and try to round them up with their loot still on them?'

'Because that's what they're paid for.'

'But that last scrap they had up there in the hills, there was real shooting. They brought down two wounded men, really wounded.'

'Well, the smugglers are very good shots. I think the Guardias Civiles mean well, but they oughtn't to carry duty to excess. If they will go potting at smugglers who can hide better than they can and shoot better than they can ...'

'You know,' said Florence after a thoughtful pause, 'I don't say anything about smugglers in my letters to people back home any more. I did at first, and stuck close to facts, too, but they

143

didn't take it so well. I guess it does read like fiction. But those two wounded men weren't fiction. No. One of them's walking about the village now, over in Estronella there, with his head all bandaged up. I bet he believes in smugglers. And so do all those British high-ups on the Rock. They haven't got your Spanish outlook.'

'They got some fine horses,' said Woolly, whose mind worked along one track. 'What do they smuggle?'

'Tobacco, chiefly,' said Lorna. 'And spirits. But people who don't know this part of Spain, don't understand; they take the worst possible view.'

'Drugs and what not?' asked Florence.

'I suppose so.'

'Well, that's silly, but that's better than thinking, as people back home do, that somebody's making it all up. And bandits, Lorna. Try to make them believe that bandits raid these farms round here, and see what they say. I just don't tell them any more. But I don't blame them. I suppose when they read my letters about smugglers and bandits in a civilized—well, a comparatively civilized place like Canada, they're entitled to think I'm showing off. I wrote and told somebody that the Government pays farmers in this district a subsidy for farming here at all, to compensate them for the—the—'

'Depredations.'

'Yes, those of the bandits, and did they believe me?'

'No, I suppose not,' said Lorna. 'But it makes sense here. And it used to make sense in England, too, in the old days in Cornwall, where nearly every man in the place knew and approved of what was going on, and the only dissenting noises came from the Excise men.'

'Does Nicholas listen to what his father tells him?'

'Certainly not,' said Lorna indignantly. 'After all, he's grown up.'

'To my mind,' said Florence sagely, 'it all hinges on whether Carmela listens to what *her* father tells *her*.'

'Don't worry,' said Lorna. 'I have some influence there, too.'

'Ah!' said Florence, and the sound was like the snort of an old war horse. 'Then let's count the odds. You're for Nicholas and so am I. That makes two of us. Two against, let me see, Don Manrique and his wife and—'

'I'm not sure which side she's on. She likes Nicholas, I think, but—'

'Well, we'll count her, anyway. You say all Carmela's relations are against the match?'

'As one man.'

'Well, we'll allow a dozen for that.'

'Make it three dozen, and it'll be slightly more accurate.'

'Three dozen. And the law-abiding British authorities over at Gibraltar. Haven't they got

145

any sporting instinct? You wouldn't think, would you, Lorna, that grown men would sneak off and tell the admiral about it, and the admiral sneak off to tell Nicholas' father? Well, allow a dozen of the British. Three dozen and one dozen, four dozen, plus Don Manrique and his wife. That makes exactly fifty against us two.'

'Fifty-one.'

'Who's the odd one?'

'Nicholas' father.'

'You think he'll matter at all?'

'No,' said Lorna. 'I don't. But count him in.'

'Count me in, too,' said Woolly.

Lorna smiled at him.

'On which side?' she asked him.

'Why, on the winning side,' said Woolly.

CHAPTER TEN

There was no need for Lorna to invite Roderick to the Casa del Carmen. His Excellency the Governor, hearing of the arrival at Gibraltar of his old schoolmate, put the fact beside his recently acquired knowledge of Lorna's previous marriage and drew an entirely erroneous conclusion. He sent an A.D.C. to the Rock Hotel with orders to bring Roderick and his luggage back with him, and applied himself genially to the task of furthering what he took to be Roderick's plans. A telephone call to Lorna on the following day informed her that His Excellency was passing that morning and would take advantage of her standing invitation to lunch. He would bring with him his old friend, Roderick Saracen.

The strength and warmth of Roderick's protests merely convinced his well-wishers of the correctness of their guess; the fellow would have to say that, naturally. Man of that type, went the general opinion, obviously wouldn't let people in on what he was after. Hid his feelings under that cold stare, but he couldn't deceive his old friends. So the official car drove through the wide-open gates, and Roderick found himself drinking Lorna's sherry and listening to his sons' respectful remarks on the view. He was introduced to the other guests, among them a personable naval captain, and noted that he seemed to be on terms of easy friendliness with his hostess. Roderick grew angry and uncomfortable, and his grey eyes became colder. He wouldn't be persuaded to repeat this farce.

His friends, however, had other ideas. The fellow, they said, in good-natured conference, needed a hand. He had come out with great hopes but insufficient courage, and it was no use letting him hang about the Rock, brooding. The thing was to give him a hand and see that he got out there to see her. The uprise of interest in his welfare found Roderick unprepared, and its weight made protest both difficult and unprofitable. He was conducted to the Casa del Carmen, unwilling but helpless, and his discomfort was little tempered by the knowledge that Lorna deplored the well-meant interference fully as much as he did.

Between Roderick and Florence, there was instant and immovable dislike. She thought him an aggressive-looking man with a domineering manner and a marked talent for polite insults. He thought her, simply, a painted hag; the cost of the paint and the modishness of the haggardness, alike passed him by. He resented her permanence based on nothing better than liking for Lorna and the house; she was deeply suspicious of his intentions and fearful of his effect upon Lorna. She would have liked to pass some of her suspicions on to Lorna, but she hesitated, and while she was hesitating, Roderick, who never had any qualms about saying what he wanted to say, was putting forward his views.

'What d'you let that woman hang on here for?' he asked Lorna.

They were alone in the drawing-room. He had been brought by friends, and the friends had tactfully withdrawn and driven away, leaving him to make the most of his opportunities. He was now making the most of them.

'Do you mean Florence?' asked Lorna,

coldly. 'If you do, she's certainly not "hanging on."'

'If I went to stay with anybody for a week or two, and was still there eight months later,' stated Roderick, 'I daresay my host wouldn't hesitate to apply the term to me. I was always told that the Spanish are great people for proverbs, but the only Spanish proverb I ever learnt was the one about fish and guests smelling equally high after the third day. Perhaps Mrs. van Leyte hasn't heard that one.'

'I think that's an extremely offensive thing to say.'

'I'm not saying anything disparaging about your guests. I'm merely trying to help you. You were never a woman who could speak up when there was any unpleasantness to be said. It may be kind-heartedness, or it may not; with you, I used to find that it was simply a lack of moral courage. You used to keep incompetent servants simply because they meant well, or looked nice about the place, or because you imagined they wouldn't get as comfortable a billet elsewhere. Or because you couldn't screw yourself up to the point of giving them notice. I suspect that's why you've got a staff in this place that must run you into a fantastic sum in salaries—and all of them doing jobs that overlap. It doesn't take two grown men to hang up my hat when I call. I could say a good deal more, but I don't want to be accused of being interfering.'

149

'I've run this house quite successfully for about eight years.'

'I don't know what you call successfully,' said Roderick morosely.

He was a man who was used to the minimum number of servants, each with a definite task which he was expected to perform faithfully. The sight of the numerous silent, smiling servitors at the Casa del Carmen caused him endless torture; he counted and re-counted all those who came into view, guessed at their wages and did prodigies of anguished mental arithmetic. It was not his money, he acknowledged, but money was money whoever owned it, and wicked waste was wicked waste and his maternal grandmother had always maintained that it ought to be made a punishable offence, and he agreed with her. This was a large house and it needed a large staff, but it didn't need an army. Meals were meals and nobody enjoyed them more than he did, but with a world shortage of food, nobody had any business to serve five courses at dinner. A dining-room, moreover, was a dining-room and people should eat in it, and not on terraces and under vines and in any other place where the view happened to be looking nice. Guests were guests and hospitality was a splendid thing, but there was no need to have the place littered with senior naval officers who appeared to have nothing to do but improve their already too friendly relations with their hostess. How Lorna could stomach that Captain Freeman—an oaf if ever he saw one—was more than he could understand. And there was this woman called Florence, who had taken root, and there was her brother, living out there in that Swiss Family Robinson manner; then there was that secretary with the rasping voice and an air of being the owner of the house putting up with rather unsatisfactory tenants.

Stephanie was seldom seen. Since Lorna's family had grown, she had been spending a great deal of time with friends at Málaga who were, she told Lorna, intellectuals. She was present at lunch on Roderick's third visit, and spoke fluently and without pause on the history of the gitanos in Spain. Roderick made several determined efforts to get a word in, but Stephanie drove on relentlessly until Lorna allowed her tablenapkin to slip off her knee, when there was a check while Stephanie waited for Natalio to pick it up and hand it to Carlos, who brought it to Stephanie, who gave it back to Lorna.

'Did you fly to Gibraltar?' she asked Roderick, at the beginning of this little pantomime.

Roderick informed her somewhat brusquely that flying was not one of his accomplishments. He was about to add grimly that he had, in point of fact, come by air, when he saw that her attention was not on him. The others, glad of

151

the opportunity of hearing their own voices, took up the conversation animatedly.

'I like the ground best,' said Florence.

'What, really?' asked Nicholas in surprise.

'Yes. I fly when I have to,' she said, 'but I'm always scared, and I think that except for the taking off and coming down again, it's just dull. Shut up in a cigar box.'

'Ten thousand feet up,' said Roderick in a reminiscent tone to nobody in particular. 'Three hundred miles an hour, and in a pressurized cabin. I didn't know I was moving.'

'That was a bad s-smash in the paper this morning,' commented Martin.

'Yes. Overcrowded runways,' said Roderick. 'They—'

'Of course, you're joking,' said Stephanie, returning without warning.

'Chocking?' Roderick stared at her in bewilderment.

'*Joking*,' she repeated.

'I am certainly not joking,' said Roderick angrily.

'I am sure,' said Stephanie severely, 'that I heard you say you didn't—'

'You don't think I'd joke about a subject like an air smash, do you?' he enquired coldly.

'I was talking about flying,' she said.

'And so was I, and I wasn't joking,' said Roderick.

'Stephanie, you skipped a b-beat,' explained

Martin.

Nicholas, avoiding his brother's glance, gathered the knotted threads, decided not to unravel them, and cut them neatly. Lorna relaxed gratefully, and gave her mind to something that had been worrying her since she walked down to visit Woolly earlier that morning. She had gone down with Martin, who had appeared to see nothing amiss, but she had an odd feeling that Woolly's manner, which had lately been calm and placid and— except when he looked directly at her— completely easy, had undergone a subtle change. She would have said, almost, that he looked frightened. It was absurd, since there was nothing here to frighten him, but all the same, there was something in his eyes—it would be ridiculous to talk about a hunted look.

It was, however, a hunted look.

Woolly's first reaction, upon meeting Roderick, had been one of frank admiration; he had not seen so splendid a figure, he confided to Martin, since, as a small boy, he had peeped through a hole in a circus tent and gazed spellbound—until forcibly removed—at the first half of the act of a magnificent long-coated, high-booted performer known as Charlie the Cossack. Of the two, he thought Roderick was perhaps the wider, but it was a close thing.

He entertained no qualms as to Roderick's

kindly interest in any business schemes he and Martin might devise, and when Florence, who had no delusion, told her brother of his strong opposition, the words, for a time, had no effect. Woolly's brain was at rest; he had made a notable effort to understand why Florence had brought him to the Casa del Carmen, and when he had understood, he had done his best to please her and had gone on to find, to his delight, that he was pleasing himself. He and Martin got along; they enjoyed their talks very much down there in the wooded patch. They would work out something—one day. They had started off well, and they were good friends; when they had the business all worked out, they would go to Martin's father and lay the thing before him and get his approval.

When at last Woolly understood that approval might not be forthcoming, he felt that his sister must be mistaken. But she was not, she insisted, in any way mistaken. Nobody was mistaken, except those who expected fatherly feeling in an ox.

'I think you're wrong, Flo,' said Woolly reproachfully. 'Why would he want to stop the boy from doing what he wants to do?'

'Because he thinks gardens ought to grow, that's why, and even if he didn't, he'd stop it because he's a big bully.'

'Bully, Flo?'

'Bully. I don't suppose he'd stop at anything to get his own way.'

154

'But see here, Flo, Marty and I have been talking about how we might get things fixed up some time.'

'You've taken long enough,' commented Florence. 'If you'd listened to me, you'd have had them fixed up long ago, and fixed up so tight that nobody could unfix them. As it is, when he finds out you've been encouraging Martin, there'll be trouble.'

'Trouble.'

'Real trouble. And it'll be aimed right at you.'

'Not me,' said Woolly, in simple faith. 'I haven't done anything. Why should he be mad at me?'

'Because he's one of these trouble-makers, and when people like making trouble, they've got to make it for somebody, haven't they? It stands to reason. He's come all the way out here from England to see what those boys are doing and to stop them from doing it, and when he knows that you've been out there with Martin, cooking up something that he doesn't approve of, he'll let himself go.'

'But it wasn't my idea, Flo. It was your idea.'

'Of course it was my idea, Woolly, but he can't do anything to me, don't you see.'

'Why not?'

'Because I'm a woman. You're a man, so he'll take it out on you. So if you take my advice, when he goes after you, just sit quiet and don't say anything about it to him.'

'But if it so happens that he'll walk up to me and ask me right out?'

'Then tell him to go away and mind his own business.'

'I don't think I could act kind of high-handed like that, Flo. He could turn round and say, "This *is* my business," just like that. What do I say then?'

'You say, "Well, smarty, you just keep out of the way and don't interfere where you're not wanted." That's all.'

'Florence, couldn't you tell him?'

'How can I tell him? He'll be talking to you, not to me.'

'You're better at coming out straight with a thing like that, Flo. You tell him, hmm?'

Woolly's 'hmm,' which would have melted a heart of stone, had no effect whatsoever upon Florence.

'It's no use asking me to tell him anything, Woolly,' she said. 'He looks at me as though he'd like to pick me up between his thumb and his finger and carry me to the door and drop me outside. He'd do it, too, if it weren't for Lorna. No, you're the one who's fixing up this thing with Martin, and you've just got to keep his father off.'

'But Flo, I can't do that!'

'Why not? You're not afraid of him, are you?' demanded Florence.

'Yes,' said Woolly.

He was very much afraid. His conviction

had always been that trouble looked a good deal less ugly when it was a long way away. Some troubles, of course, had to be faced, but not this trouble. This was one of those troubles that could be, that should be, that would be avoided. A big man like that, reasoned Woolly, could do a lot of damage if he was thoroughly roused. There wasn't, he calculated, peering at Roderick from behind a convenient pillar, a flabby muscle in his whole body. The man was hard and fighting fit. And he had a jaw that didn't promise well for anybody who went up to him and spoke right out, as Florence advised. This was an ugly customer, and a wise man would keep out of his way.

Woolly, therefore, retreated to his home and stayed there, refusing every invitation to come over to the house for lunch or dinner. He was safer, he mused, where he was. If anybody wanted to see him, they knew where to come. He could see them coming, too. If he didn't want people to find him at home, all he had to do was skip out and cut through the trees and get behind one of the thicker trunks. He was better equipped for hiding behind tree trunks than some he could name.

Woolly stayed in his own domain, and Florence stayed prudently in her own rooms and Stephanie, after engaging in one or two contests of brain versus brawn and finding that brain had the worst of it, retired to her room and took up the study of Swedish. The kindly

157

and well-intentioned friends who had taken Roderick to the Casa del Carmen found excuses to withdraw and leave him there alone, and thus the circle narrowed and became a family circle, with the occasional additions of the more hardy members of Lorna's circle who could withstand the cold of Roderick's glance and manner. The two hardiest were Captain Freeman, who was too deeply in love with Lorna to give way to anything less than a dismissal from her, and an old friend named Bill Charton, an intrepid man who gave Roderick stare for stare and dared him silently to try and make something of it if he cared to. His yacht lay out to sea not two hundred yards from the Casa del Carmen, it seemed to the irritated Roderick as he watched the neat dinghy go to and fro.

Nicholas was making his own plans, and he divulged some of them to his father when the latter arrived at the house one morning just as Nicholas and Martin were on the point of going out. Nicholas paused on the porch.

'Dad—'

'Well?'

'I'm arranging to get a spot of leave, and Mother's asking Carmela to come and stay down here. Will you—'

'I suppose I shall have to meet her,' said Roderick, 'but what I want to do first is have a word with her father.'

'What did he say?' asked Martin, when

Nicholas joined him in the car.

'Not much. Says he wants to see the father, not the daughter. Funny, isn't it, how parents take it on themselves to forbid you to marry somebody they've never set eyes on. If that isn't prejudice in its lowest and most lurid guise, then—'

'The objection isn't p-personal,' pointed out Martin consolingly. 'It's—well, take you and Don Manrique. He and I got talking about you on that ride. He's got nothing against you, just as Father's got nothing specific agaisnt Carmela. But they've both got someone else in mind, and that acts like a b-beam in the eye. Don Manrique's hankering after a chap who's a distant relation of some sort, and Father's trying to tie you up to that girl over at Winchelsea. After all, you did give him the idea that your intentions were what he'd call honourable.'

'I took her out a few times, that's all.'

'Yes, but there was that week-end at Henley.'

'With her brother and his wife.'

'Yes, technically. But from Father's point of view, rather final.'

'What do you think of Carmela?'

'Carmela? She's rather pretty, I think.'

'*Rather* pretty! Good Lord!'

'Well, lovely, then. I didn't see for long, remember. I was out with her father most of the time. Nick—'

'What?'

'Those yarns about her father and his bit of s-smuggling on the side—'

'What about them?'

'I was just wondering. You see, Don Manrique took me out on a long ride the other day. It's d-damn decent of him to let me ride his horses, but, well, something on that ride made me wonder.'

'If there was anything in the wind,' said Nicholas, 'he wouldn't have risked taking you.'

'But there was nothing for the eye to see. It was just that is struck me that the whole idea of the ride seemed to be pointless. He wasn't out for exercise, and neither were the horses. I was quite c-certain that the horses knew where they were going.'

'Nothing remarkable in that.'

'No, but I think Don Manrique went out to look for something. I couldn't p-prove it, of course, but that was my idea.'

'You might be right. They smuggle stuff by a kind of obstacle-relay-race method. So many men ride so far on so many horses, and when they reach a nice, quiet, pre-arranged spot up in the mountains, they hand the swag over to the next lot of fellows waiting with the next lot of horses. There might be something in the wind. There must be something keeping him at Yago, or I think he would have taken Carmela away and kept her out of reach until I'd left.'

'Well, I think he was choosing a site for the next lot of operations.'

'Perhaps that's why he's allowing Carmela to come down and stay with mother. If he's going to be away, I suppose he feels it doesn't matter whether I see her up there or down here.'

Lorna was saying almost the same thing at the same moment.

'Don Manrique's going to be away for a time,' she told Roderick. 'In any case, why don't you see the girl first?'

'It seems I'm going to. I understand from Nicholas that she's coming to stay here next week when he gets his leave.'

'Yes.'

'They appear to be getting a great deal of assistance from you,' he observed.

'They are.'

'Well, I suppose you know what you're doing. Do you really think that his marriage to the daughter of an obscure Spanish farmer, and a smuggler into the bargain, is going to improve his chances in life?'

'My dear Roderick, Don Manrique isn't obscure and he isn't a farmer. His family is older and nobler than yours, and he merely chooses to live quietly in the country. His daughter is beautiful, very well educated and very well brought up. No girl, of whatever nationality, could make him a more suitable wife.'

161

He looked at her. The words were spoken without emphasis; they came with Lorna's normal, unhurried air. She was sitting on a window seat in the drawing-room, and her hands were folded quietly on her lap. Most of the shades in the room were lowered against the sun's rays, giving an effect of cool quietness in keeping with her demeanor. He acknowledged, with detachment, that she made a lovely picture, and went on to clear his mind of some of the resentment he had been building up against her.

'That's a matter of opinion,' he said. 'In any case, you might have sounded me on the matter.'

'Nicholas has already sounded you on the matter. You'd been listening to a lot of silly stories in your club, and you got the idea that Carmela's father was a sort of desperado. Nothing could be more ridiculous. He's a gentleman, and a charming one. I hope you won't go up to Yago with the idea that you're going to meet anybody less cultured than yourself.'

'The man must have some sense; he's as much against this engagement as I am.'

'He had other plans for his daughter.'

'Well, I hope he'll be able to carry them out. If you know Nicholas as well as I do, you'll realize that getting himself entangled with girls is one of his hobbies.'

'Don't imagine he isn't serious this time. He

162

is, and so am I. I've known Carmela since she was a child, even if I haven't known Nicholas. She's sweet and good, and she's just right for him.'

'Why don't you let him go home and marry a decent English girl? Why saddle him with a foreign wife and foreign in-laws? Take your own case: you're the daughter of a mixed marriage of that kind, and look at you now, out here among foreigners, living their life, speaking their language and never even feeling the urge to go back and take a look at your own people. You're an Englishwoman; it doesn't matter what your mother was. You were born an Englishwoman and you had an Englishman for a father, and if he'd had any sense, he would have made certain that you'd stay in your own country, instead of being allowed to roam about, pulling up your roots as soon as you put them down. Nicholas thought you were Spanish before he met you; I don't understand how you can lose your identity as completely as that.'

'I've simply elected to live with my mother's—and my husband's—people, that's all.'

'You didn't show such a deep sense of duty towards your first husband.'

She made no reply. They looked at one another, and he found himself, for once, obeying an impulse.

'Were you happy?' he asked.

Her eyebrows went up.

'With Juan?'

He merely nodded, feeling slightly ill. How she could tie herself up with a fellow called Hoo-arn.

'Was he good to you?' he asked.

'Very good. You ruined his life, you know. He was deeply in love; he was to have been married, and you ruined it all.'

'No, I didn't,' he said steadily. 'That's what you told Nicholas, and it isn't the truth. The truth is that everything happened at once and made a stupid, tragic muddle, that's all. My sisters—'

'Were jealous.'

'They were nothing of the sort. They merely felt that you were behaving with less discretion than a wife should. I felt that you needed a firm hand. You felt that my letter was a cold and reasoned accusation. Your mother felt that it was too late to prevent a separation. Salvador knew that his own affair was finished and that his only honourable course lay in marrying you. When you look back dispassionately, you can see that we all behaved with something considerably less than sense. But it's over.'

'Yes,' agreed Lorna, 'it's over, but unless you're careful, you're going to be the cause of upsetting everything all over again. It was a mistake to come out here, and it's a mistake to suppose that there's anything wrong with Carmela or her father. I think your wisest

164

course would be to go home quietly and—'

'And leave Martin to talk himself into some crackpot scheme with that Canadian fellow out there? My dear Lorna, you must think me a very inadequate father.'

There was a pause, during which he realized that he had used her name, and in a tone of exasperation. With a strong effort, he forced himself to speak with what he felt was sweet reasonableness.

'Don't encourage them, Lorna. I warn you, I'm not going to stand by and watch you giving them everything they think they want. If you and I take a united stand, we'll have Nicholas out of this, and Martin too, and things will work themselves out.'

'How?'

'Nicholas will find a girl of his own nationality, and Martin can get down to a serious job.'

'In England?'

'Certainly in England. They can come out and visit you whenever you wish, when they've got leave and so on. And if you care to take a holiday yourself in England at any time, I'll go away for a time and put the house at your disposal.'

'You're very kind.'

'Not at all.'

'And rather misguided.'

'That's a matter of opinion.'

'And completely and utterly pig-headed.'

165

'Thank you.'

'You are,' said Lorna, in a conversational tone, 'the most rigid, the most hidebound and insanely obstinate man I ever met. Your own ideas and your own opinions suffice for you; nobody else's have any weight or even any interest. You make up your mind and then you keep it made up.'

'I make it up after a good deal of thought. I know what's best for those two boys. You haven't seen them for nearly twenty years, and it's natural that when you do, you should try to please them by handing them everything they ask for on a plate, regardless of whether it's something they should have or not. You've lost touch with solid people; you've lived too long with these mañana Johnnies. You live in ease and luxury. You've grown used to hothouse conditions and you can't realize that a week of this sort of thing would rot the fibres of anybody trained to a more rigorous system. Already I can see its effects on the two boys.'

'Certainly you can. Martin has put on five pounds and looks comparatively well fed.'

'He looked perfectly all right before he got here.'

'He looked appalling. And his glasses hadn't been changed for ten years. And his clothes looked as though they hadn't, either. He looked thin and lost and neglected.'

'Nonsense.'

'He needs help. And so does Nicholas.'

166

'Utter nonsense.'

'And I shall do my best to give it to them. I shall—are you leaving?'

'Yes, I am. Thank you for your hospitality. Let me make it clear that I don't want to thrust myself on you, but if coming here is the only way I can get hold of Nicholas and Martin, then I shall be reluctantly compelled to come here until I can persuade them that they'll both be better elsewhere. Good-bye.'

'Adios,' said Lorna, tranquilly.

He was driven away towards Gibraltar, and he noted, as he drove through the gates, that they stood open. He wondered who was expected and was not long in ignorance, for as his own car swung into the road, another entered the Casa del Carmen, and Roderick recognized the figure at the wheel and uttered a low and growling curse.

Freeman. Gates wide open, and Lorna wearing a dress obviously designed to kill. Martin had said something ... 'Mother finds him amusing.' So he was on his way in there now to be amusing. Then that other fellow with the yacht would row himself across ...

The contrast between his own cool leave-taking and the warm welcome his imagination accorded the captain did nothing to relieve the gloom that had descended on his spirits. His was not a disposition that could be called merry, but he was, as a rule, at peace with himself and of a fairly even temper. He had a

167

home he liked in a country he loved. He had lived a hard and active life; he had retired early, but had kept himself as fit and as hard as his work in the uplands of Kenya had done. He enjoyed a good deal of sport; he had friends and knew how to get hold of them when he wanted them. A few weeks ago, he remembered morosely, he had been a man free from care. Nicholas was giving no trouble and was going to be, for a time, in places where girls would not fall off trees for his enlivenment. Martin was in a good job. He had no servant troubles, and his income was sufficient for his needs, with a safety margin. There had been nothing to warn him that he would soon be driving along a road in the south of Spain, with his wife working against him and his sons in revolt. He had come out here to act, and to act firmly and effectively, and he found himself forced into a position which, after some deep thought, he could only liken to that of an interloper in a modern Eden. His wife was behaving treacherously and his sons were disloyal, and he was doing nothing, and he wished very much that he could shed his responsibilities and go home.

He looked round at the scenes through which he was passing, his habitual distrust of tourist propaganda heightened by an uprising of acute homesickness. Sapphire sea. Yes, it was over there, for those who wanted it. Local colour. Plenty: grown men sitting on overworked little donkeys. He'd like very much to get out and make the donkeys sit on the men. Vivid colours: he'd give it all for a sight of his slate-grey house and the gentle hills beyond. Mountain panorama: up there lived the smuggling character that Nicholas proposed to make his father-in-law. A gentleman, Lorna had called him. Old family and noble. A likely story. No doubt she believed everything she was told, but he preferred to do a little investigating. And investigate he would. He would spare himself the humiliation of visiting the Casa del Carmen, and he would go up and call upon this Fernandez fellow. And by thunder, he'd do it now.

He leaned forward and gave an order, and presently the car left the main road and turned toward the mountain. The road was bad and got worse, but Roderick was prepared to endure, and the tyres and springs were not his. It was worth everything to get up there and get a few words with this Fernandez.

Don Manrique was informed of the car's approach and studied it for a few moments through powerful glasses. It was not difficult to guess who was coming; if he had doubts, there were men standing round him who could tell him.

Roderick reached the house to find himself received courteously by a servant. His master was away; his mistress was away; it was unfortunate, but the family had gone away and would not return for some time.

Roderick drove away again, and Don Manrique watched the car and sighed. It was a long way to come for so little. But this was not the time for visitors. He had heavier matters on his hands. When the business was over, there would be time for family affairs.

CHAPTER ELEVEN

Nicholas, desiring to enjoy as much time as possible with Carmela during his period of leave, gave instructions to Martin that he was to borrow Lorna's car, drive up to Yago and bring Carmela to the Casa del Carmen at an hour that would coincide happily with Nicholas' own arrival.

The car was borrowed and Martin was preparing to set off, when there was the clatter of hooves on the drive, and Carmela herself rode up, small and straight on a large chestnut mare, with a retinue consisting of a groom, a handsome young manservant with a smiling maid perched comfortably behind him, a mule laden with several large suit-cases, and last of all, a muscular gentleman who appeared to be guarding the convoy. The whole made a pretty picture which Lorna and Florence, coming out on the porch to welcome the young guest, appreciated to the full.

'It's those red trappings I like so much,' said Lorna. 'I've seen them all my life, on and off, and they still excite me. They make a horse look gay without detracting from his dignity. And a mule, too,' she added, seeing its ears twitch expectantly.

'You could start up a dude ranch with this lot,' commented Florence. 'Will you tell me why they've brought down two extra horses?'

Carmela, riding up and dismounting, explained that her father had sent her down with two extra horses which were to be placed at the disposal of his friends Martin and Don Woolly. Martin and Woolly were informed of this, an example of true Spanish courtesy; they reacted characteristically: Martin went pale with pleasure and then red with embarrassment, and was finally understood to say that it was jolly decent of all concerned. While he was saying it, Woolly had chosen the better of the two horses for his own use. He then mounted forthwith, his long legs dangling far below the stirrups, and rode at the head of the cavalcade to the stables.

Lorna looked after him thoughtfully. It was a kind gesture, and she was grateful to Don Manrique, but she found herself wondering what, if anything, lay behind the incident. Martin had been given an open invitation to go up to Yago to ride whenever he cared to; he had no designs on Carmela, and he rode well

171

and could be trusted to look after his mounts. This presentation might mean that Don Manrique wished to place a horse at his disposal down here in order to save him the long journey to Yago; it might also mean— Lorna's eyes turned to the mountains, as though searching there for the answer—it might also mean that Don Manrique was making certain that keen-witted young men did not appear at his house, unheralded, during the next week or so. There must, she decided, be something afoot. The permission granted to Carmela had been in itself astounding, for since Nicholas' advent, no visits entailing a night at the Casa del Carmen had been permitted. But Carmela was here, and Martin's visits had been charmingly forestalled. Certainly, decided Lorna, with no feelings but those of friendly interest, Don Manrique was busy. And certainly it must be a heavier cargo than usual, to compel him to give Nicholas so free a hand.

Nicholas arrived late and ignominiously; the car had shown a strong disinclination to begin the journey at all and had sulked for half of it. It had then snorted, flounced, and tossed the larger part of its engine spitefully into the road. Reassembly would take days. Two passing donkeys were at once placed by their owners at Nicholas' disposal. He put his luggage upon one and himself upon the other. The owners of the animals walked behind carrying an assortment of metal which might or might not come together as an engine once more.

'You look sweet,' said Florence, looking at him with admiration as he rode up. 'But you ought to have a nice, big straw hat.'

'Give me time; I'm only a new donkey-boy,' said Nicholas. 'Where's Carmela?'

'I'm here,' said Carmela.

She had changed and was in white, and in the unselfconscious fashion of Spanish women, had put a red flower in her hair. She looked fresh and dainty, and had the happy air of one who has full confidence of the party coming up to her expectations of enjoyment. Nicholas picked her up, seated her in one of the flower-covered arches of the porch, and looked at her with pride.

'Hello, Nick,' said Martin, coming out with his mother. 'I didn't have to f-fetch Carmela. Her father sent her down with a horse for me. Mine. Para mi.'

'Ah, Spanish!' said Carmela. 'Say some more.'

'That's all he knows,' said Nicholas. 'Those were the first words he said in English, too. He used them whenever he grabbed my possessions.'

'He's at least trying,' pointed out Lorna. 'He bought a phrase book, which is more than you ever bothered to do.'

'Phrase books are just a waste of time,' said Nicholas.

'Not this one,' said Martin. 'The very first sentence is "You are asking too much; I will call a p-policeman." Starts you off on the right tack straight away.'

It was agreed by all that there was a helpful directness about the sentence.

'It's pretty elastic, too,' pointed out Nicholas. 'It might have a purely financial angle, and again, it might not. I've wanted to use it on several occasions and in several languages.'

'Let's go for a p-picnic,' suggested Martin. 'Is it too cold to swim?'

'That's no reason for not swimming,' said Nicholas.

'I can't swim,' Carmela reminded him.

He lifted her down with a smile. She didn't swim; she didn't play tennis or golf. She walked no more than was necessary. He thought of the wife he had had in mind: a girl who drove through the water in a steady crawl, got out and changed into a golf outfit and went out to sink putts nonchalantly from the edge of the green. He had imagined her smashing her way through Wimbledon, stopped by nothing except the American entries. She was to be a girl who was soft and yielding by night, but in good, hard trim during the day. And here was Carmela. She was small and slight in the circle of his arm as he swung her to the ground. He could span her waist between his two hands. But what she lacked in muscle, she made up in

174

fire. He would take her just as she was.

'You don't have to swim,' he told her. 'You can dabble in the cream at the edges. Come on.'

Later, Lorna, who had refused to accompany them, stood watching them as they set off. They had driven a bargain for the retention of the donkeys on a so-much-an-hour basis, and had loaded them with provisions for the picnic. Nicholas and Carmela led the way, Florence followed with Martin, and in the rear came Stephanie and Woolly, the last two unexpectedly drawn together by the discovery that they each knew ten words of Swedish.

Lorna was glad to have an opportunity for some quiet thought. She liked tranquillity, and life, lately, had been far from tranquil. A short time ago everyone had been going peacefully about their business: Florence had been a welcome guest, Stephanie a not-too-obtrusive secretary. Nicholas had found a mother and an ally; Martin had met a friend who might prove useful. She herself ... Lorna put her own feelings aside and stared thoughtfully after the disappearing figures. This was Woolly's first appearance among them since he had grasped the significance of Roderick's attitude; he had only been persuaded to join the picnic by repeated assurances that nobody would know where they were going or be able to follow them. Even Florence, lately, wore an apprehensive look. Nicholas was looking faintly worried, and Martin—perhaps, of them all, Martin was the least affected by his father's presence.

Roderick, Roderick, Roderick. It was all Roderick. He had destroyed their peace, thought Lorna angrily. He had swooped down and scattered the more timid among them into retreat. He had not come in any spirit of compromise; there was to be no discussion, no concession, nothing of give and take. He had brought his own opinions and terms, and he was still clinging to them. Everybody was to see his point and give way.

She turned and walked thoughtfully indoors and shut herself into her sitting-room to examine her position. She tried to look at matters clearly and coolly, but she found that the more clearly the facts emerged, the less cool she found herself. She realized that she had forgotten a great deal about Roderick; if she had not, she would have known that he was not a man who would remain in England and content himself with writing his wishes to his rebel sons. His prompt appearance on the scene was characteristic and ought not to have surprised her; nor should she have been dismayed by his subsequent visits, for though she herself might see him as an interfering outsider, to others, she admitted somewhat begrudgingly, he would appear a man still handsome, still attractive enough to find favour wherever he sought it. He had come, and where another man might have felt embarrassment, he had galloped into battle with a speed and a zest that showed how galling he had found the restraint imposed by distance. He was among them, causing them a great deal of discomfort and likely to cause them more. His plan was easy to read. Florence and Woolly and Stephanie were to go; Nicholas was to forget Carmela, and Martin was to return with him to England and take the first good job that offered. And she herself . . .

It was useless to deny it. It was childish to hide it away and pretend it wasn't there. It was Woollyish to go up the nearest tree and refuse to come down. It was better to drag it out and look it straight in the face. Now. Look at it; identify it; say it out loud.

'I'm frightened,' said Lorna, aloud.

But of what?

If this was to be a discussion, then let her discuss it reasonably. Aloud.

'Why,' asked Lorna of herself in the small mirror above the mantelpiece, 'why are you frightened?'

You're a grown woman, can't you find out?

Well, it's Roderick. He's—he's disturbing.

Do you mean that he disturbs you emotionally?

Oh, don't be ridiculous! Do you imagine that that great, big—

Careful, now. It's no use calling him a lout, if you were going to. There's nothing loutish about him. He's really a rather striking-looking man.

All right, I'll admit that. But I'd forgotten all about him, and I was perfectly happy, wasn't I?

You say so.

Well, I was. This house—and everything. I felt happy, and I felt safe. I felt that I was my own mistress, and that I would remain my own mistress until I—

Decided to become someone else's?

Chose to marry any one of the perfectly charming men who asked me. There was Pierre Fresnay, I could have married him.

You said he was too restless.

There was the Count, he was mad about me.

You said—I remember thinking at the time that it was rather indelicate—that he was too hairy.

Then there's Bill Charton.

Last time he put in here, you said he was the same age as yourself and that you'd prefer someone older. You said that in another ten years he'd look like your son instead of like your husband.

Then there's Captain Freeman. I've never said anything against him.

Not against him, exactly, but you did come in here one night after he'd left and say you wondered whether you'd ever feel anything again. I wasn't quite sure what you meant, but I took it to be a kind of oblique criticism.

But what I wanted to prove was that I lived a

life of what even you would admit to be free choice. If I were offered something, I could accept or refuse it. I could order my household; I could—as I said before, I could order my life. And now I feel that I can't do that any more.

Why?

Because when I'm dealing with Roderick, I get nowhere. He pauses while I say what I have to say, and then he goes on where he left off.

All men are like that.

Yes, but Roderick's worse. He doesn't even give any sign of having heard a word; if he does hear, he doesn't take the smallest notice of anything I've said. He's like a steamroller, he just rolls on. His ideas, his opinions and his intentions haven't changed one iota since he landed from that plane; you wouldn't think he was dealing with live people at all.

Why should that alarm you? He won't change Nicholas; at any given moment Nicholas will just go off and marry his Carmela. And you must admit that Martin's ideas, at the moment, aren't very clear-cut. His father's only looking into the future and trying to make it secure for him. What's frightening you? At the worst, Martin will go back to England to work, but you'll be able to see him as often as you want to. Both the boys adore you; their father can't do anything about that and probably doesn't want to. If he sends Florence and Woolly and Stephanie packing— well, what does it matter? They'd have to go at some time. It might annoy you to have their going speeded, but there's nothing frightening about that either. So do let's have it.

Well, you won't think I'm imagining it, will you?

No.

Then, I think he's—I think he—

You think he's in love with you?

No! No, no, no! But don't you understand, if he got the idea that now that Nicholas and Martin have brought me back into the family, as it were, the tidiest thing would be to become a real family again, then he'd decide to be tidy. And then what would happen to me? I've just told you that he isn't even *aware* of what other people happen to want. And when they try to tell him, he isn't interested. If he decides that we ought to be a family again, he'll make up his mind to marry me. And if he makes up his mind to marry me—You see, the appalling thing is that he *has*.

Decided to marry you?

I'm afraid so. I'm almost sure. He doesn't know it; at the moment it hasn't come home to him. But the signs are unmistakable.

What sort of signs?

I can't tell you, because there's nothing, so far, that you can put into words. But it's stark truth.

Did he say anything?

No. It was Captain Freeman who first made me think that there was something. He always

180

used to regard Roderick as harmless, as far as I was concerned. He never shared the general idea that there was anything between Roderick and myself. He was quite certain there wasn't. But lately he's changed his mind, and he watches Roderick all the time they're together, and he's wary and suspicious and thinks he's after something. And Bill Charton's the same. When he first came he used to be quite friendly with Roderick, but now he won't go near him. He says he doesn't like the way Roderick looks at me. That was the first real alarm, but after that, I saw what he meant. Roderick *is* different. He still looks cold and impersonal, and we can't talk for ten minutes without disagreeing, but something's forming in his mind. I have a terrible feeling that one day he's going to say, 'My dear Lorna, this situation is really rather ridiculous, you'd much better marry me and be done with it.' That's just how he'll say it, and nothing I can say or do— nothing, nothing, nothing—will make him understand that I haven't agreed to do it. Just because he feels it to be the sensible solution, He'll go ahead without attending to what he calls distracting comment. I'm frightened, and I'm all the more frightened because it's so nebulous. There isn't anything to put a finger on, but it's *there*.

I think I see.

I suppose you're going to accuse me of exaggerating?

No, I'm not. Far from it.

You mean you—you believe it?

Yes, I do.

You mean I've—I've convinced you?

Completely.

Then you're—you're frightened, too?

Yes. We're of one mind.

CHAPTER TWELVE

Roderick was driving out to the Casa del Carmen. It was dusk, and he was in eveing dress, for he had been invited to dine.

Lorna's invitation had been verbal, and had been uttered without any kind of preliminary as he was about to leave her house, two days earlier.

'Will you come and have dinner with us on Thursday?'

He had experienced a sudden rush of longing: to come out as a guest, invited, and invited with the first touch of warmth she had shown since his arrival. A wave of eagerness rose in him and then broke against the rock of distaste: those fellows would be there— Freeman and the one off the yacht, and probably a whole menagerie more. No, he wouldn't come and have dinner on Thursday, or any other day. He opened his mouth to say so.

'Have you forgotten that it's Martin's birthday?'

Yes, he had. Clean forgotten. That was bad; he didn't remember birthdays as a general rule, but he had a little book in which he noted down the more important ones, and so far he'd managed to glance at it in time to avoid giving disappointment to his sons. He'd forgotten.

'Thank you,' he said stiffly. 'What time?'

'Any time,' said Lorna. 'The Spanish dinner hour—about ten, but come as early as you like.'

'I suppose it's a—I suppose you're giving a party of some kind, with—'

'No. Martin wanted as few people as possible. Florence is being very kind and taking Stephanie on a sight-seeing trip to Granada. They'll be away for three days. Woolly isn't going with them, but he won't join us, so that leaves you and the boys—and, of course, Carmela will be here.'

Carmela. She was staying in the house, but she had not been in when he called; she and Nicholas had driven out for the day.

'I suppose it's time I met her,' he said.

'Quite time,' said Lorna.

He had intended to be early, but his plans had not gone well. He had had an idea for a present for Martin, but it had meant going over to Tangier. That put the price of it up somewhat, but it was worth it—though it didn't look it, in its unpretentious box beside

183

the chauffeur. It had delayed him considerably; the sun was already low, and it would be almost dark when he reached the Casa del Carmen. It was a pity, but it couldn't be helped. He gave orders to the driver to proceed as rapidly as discretion allowed, and settled himself in the back of the car with some impatience. This, he felt, was scarcely the birthday he would have planned for Martin. This Arabian Nights environment was all very well for those who liked it, but for himself, he would have preferred to take the boy up to London for a celebration of some kind. This was a poor substitute; not the food or the wine, against which he had not a word to say, apart from its lavishness—but something more homelike would have suited him a great deal better.

They were nearing the house when Roderick caught sight of something that held his attention for a moment. Something brought him upright in his seat, but when he identified the figure he had seen, he could not account for the feeling of urgency that had, for a moment, seized him. It was nothing; a man on a horse. He'd been dreaming as he passed, and his training simply told him that the animal was one of exceptional quality—that was all.

But it wasn't all, argued a small voice within him. There was something else, if only he could get his mind round to it. A man on a horse, making his way quietly up into the mountains.

184

A man on a—and then, suddenly, Roderick knew who the man was. He was the man who had received him when he had paid the abortive visit to Don Manrique's house at Yago. That was the man; that was the fellow who'd come out and said with every appearance of truth that his master was away for an indefinite period. The little problem was solved, but the sense of urgency remained. Why, Roderick wondered, was he making so much of the sight of a man on a horse?

He twisted himself round in his seat and peered out of the back of the car. But the car had rounded a curve and there was nothing to be seen but the steep side of a hill. Then, as they swung once more on to an open stretch of road, Roderick found what he was looking for. The man on the horse—but now there were two. And above them, shadowy against the dark hills and invisible to any but an eye trained to the keenness of Roderick's, was a third.

He turned back thoughtfully. He would have given a great deal to stop the car and direct a powerful pair of glasses on the figures of the three men, but the light was almost gone and time was going too; he did not carry powerful fieldglasses when he went out to dinner, and he was already late for his appointment. There was probably, he mused, a nice little bit of dirty work going on at the local cross-roads, but it was nothing to do with him—or it wouldn't be unless Nicholas married into the smuggling fraternity. His mind roamed with keen interest over the probable scope of the night's work. They said that those horses knew the job; they were trained to it. They were shown the course beforehand, and then all their riders had to do—when the appointed night came, and the loads were aboard—was to settle down in the saddle and let the horses find their own way.

The dark, secret mountains frowned down, and Roderick frowned back. Those fellows had it too much their own way. He'd give something to get out and go after them.

The car drew up with a suddenness that jerked Roderick's head forward.

'What the—?'

The car was a military one, lent to Roderick for the journey to the Casa. The driver, an intelligent young Cockney, spoke over his shoulder to his passenger.

'Sorry, sir.'

'What is it?'

'Guardias Civiles, sir. Civil Guards, as you might say. They're goin' up into the mountains.'

'On the prowl?' asked Roderick.

'No, sir. Not this time. There's a bit of excitement tonight, sir. I got the news at La Linea when we was waiting to come through. These police chaps have had wind of a little bit of smuggling that's going on tonight, and they're off after 'em.'

186

'Who gives those fellows away?'

'Nobody gives them away, sir. But this game goes on all the time. The police watch the contraband boys, and when they think they're moving the stuff, sir, then they go after 'em. Tonight's the night, as you might say, sir.'

Roderick leaned forward to stare out at the cavalcade passing the car. Four, eight, ten, twelve of them. 'Twelve Guardias Civiles,' muttered Roderick exultingly to himself. Twelve of those chaps with those shiny, folded-paper hats, crossing the main road and cutting up into one of those mule tracks that led into the mountains. They were on the scent. They were on the hunt; good luck to them.

The riders clattered across the road and the horses' hooves became muffled and then died away as they gained the side of the hill and began to climb. The car moved forward once more, but Roderick's head was screwed round and his eyes were stabbing the darkness to see the last of the horses and their uniformed riders.

Carbines! They were always armed, of course, but that lot seemed to have an air of purpose. The hunt was up! He had been right; something was going on. There was going to be a game of hide and seek up there in the darkness, and those chaps with the hats were ... God! thought Roderick, yearningly, I'd give a lot to be in on that. A dark ride, and a scenting of the quarry; a round-up and a

187

triumphant return. I'd give a lot.

But he wasn't going on a mountain chase, he remembered. He was going to dinner. He was going to a party. He was on his way, not into the dark, remote heights to chase smugglers, but to a dinner-party—an engagement of a less spectacular kind. Here was no dark rendezvous of smugglers, but the light over the entrance to the Casa del Carmen.

The gate was open; the second gate was being opened, and Roderick, in the car, would have passed through it and so to his son's birthday party if it had not been for the fact that his ears were as keen as his eyes. Above the purr of the engine, above the clamour of the gate-keepers and the creak of one gate closing and the clang of another opening, he heard the whinny of a horse. And before the car, which had paused before the iron gate, could move on again, Roderick had opened the door and was issuing a curt order to the driver.

'Drop me here,' he said. 'And I shan't want you again tonight. I'll make my own arrangements for getting back.'

'Very good, sir.'

Roderick watched the car turn and drive away; then he turned and walked swiftly in the direction of the stables, his thoughts racing. He was making a fool of himself, but that didn't matter. Nicholas had told him that there were two horses in those stables that belonged to that Manrique fellow. They probably knew what was going on just as clearly as though they were up there with their companions. He, Roderick, was going to throw a blanket over the back of one of them to protect his evening trousers and—fool or no fool—he was going to ride a mile with those chaps in the shiny hats. They wouldn't let him go far, true, but for a few moments, he'd be where he longed to be—out in the open with a decent animal under him ... on the hunt.

There was only one horse in the stables, but one was all he needed. Roderick felt grateful, for the first time, to the Spanish instinct for taking things as they came. The small boys in temporary charge of the stables while the grooms ate their evening meal saw nothing unduly odd about an Englishman in evening dress straddling a horse and riding at a smart pace into the darkness.

Some instinct warned Roderick to avoid the main gate and go to the small, wooden door by which the servants came and went. They might let him out—or they might not. It depended on how much they knew, and he was prepared to gamble on their knowing a good deal. But there was nobody at the gate, and soon he was through it and across the road. The horse gave a snort of pleasure and took the first ascent at a pace that made it necessary for Roderick to apply all the known and some of the unknown principles of horsemanship in order to keep his seat. They rose, swerved and rose again, and

189

Roderick bent low as branches loomed up and passed over him, stroking his back affectionately as they went.

For the first time since leaving England, he was completely happy. The impulse had been a rash one, but in obeying it he seemed to have shed the vague discomfort that had centred round his heart for the past weeks. He felt alive and clear-headed, and matters seemed to fall, there in the darkness, into their proper perspective.

He found himself clasping the horse affectionately round the neck, and disengaged himself hastily. The animal had come to an abrupt halt, and Roderick, sensing its complete immobility, knew that it had heard something, and was waiting to hear it again. In the dead, eerie silence of the night, horse and man listened, and then suddenly Roderick looked up and saw outlined against the sky for a brief moment the figures of the Guardias Civiles he had seen on the road below.

Roderick put his heels to his horse—once, and then again. And as he dug them in for the third time and felt the animal's steady resistance to his urging, the truth became clear: the horse knew and recognized the enemy, and no persuasion and no force could compel him to join them. Roderick, between admiration and disappointment, realized that he was beaten, and turned for home.

The horse turned obediently—and that was

the last direction it obeyed. Roderick found that, far from dropping to the level of the road, they were rising, rising rapidly, silently in darts and swerves and neck-jolting jerks. Something that might be a light from the Casa de Nuestra Señora del Carmen shone at a distance that Roderick did not care to estimate. He rode grimly and realized with appalling clarity that he could either stay on the horse and go with it to what he had decided would be its own stable at Don Manrique's house, or he could disembark and walk down to his dinner engagement. It was a poor choice and not worth considering. He had been crazy to come on this expedition at all, but he had been criminally stupid to embark upon it riding a powerful and spirited animal on a snaffle. He had no hope of exerting control, and it was only by exercising all his wit and muscle that he could manage to stay on the animal at all.

They rose to a point at which the woods thinned, and Roderick realized that the visibility was slightly better. Any satisfaction this might have caused him was checked abruptly as he looked down and saw that the horse was moving along a path no more than six feet wide, with a steep mountain on one side and on the other a sheer, sickening drop. Roderick, peering ahead, saw to his horror that the path went on for a few yards more and then vanished, and his stomach contracted as he felt, rather than saw before him, a black, unfathomable void. He tried to close his eyes, only to find that they remained open and staring. A stabbing flash of memory brought back, in as many seconds, three terrible tales of horses and riders that had plunged to their death. He waited with the calm of desperation—and then he found that the horse had swung round at a sharp angle. His hindquarters seemed to hang for an agonizing moment in space, and then they were on solid ground once more, following the path along the other side of the mountain, rising, rising and at times, it seemed to Roderick, clawing their way up the sheer side and hanging giddily over nothingness.

His mind, swept of all save the mortal necessity of staying on the horse, lost count of time and distance. This was the cost of a moment's recklessness and folly. He had asked for this.

They were not, he saw, climbing now. They were on a level path and the horse was picking its way over a broken and rocky surface. Roderick looked round, looked back, and found that a suspicion which had been forming dimly in his mind was now a certainty: they were not making for Don Manrique's house. They were a considerable distance away from it, and a considerable height above it.

Roderick made a last desperate attempt to check his mount. The horse went on, and then slowed and seemed to feel his way. The beautiful head went up, and Roderick found his own nostrils twitching as though through this sense he could pierce the blackness that had defeated sight. They were near something; what, he couldn't tell, but the horse knew.

'Who's that,' he said, in a voice which something warned him to keep low.

There was a pause, and then a familiar, drawling voice came through the darkness.

'Well, now!' said Woolly.

'What in hell,' said Roderick, 'do you think you're doing up here.'

'I'm not doing anybody a mite of harm,' said Woolly. 'All I'm doing, I'm seeing how these smuggler chaps find their way round up here. I saw them—I've got a kind of look-out—and I've been watching them all day, off and on, and I said to myself, "Now, what's all this?" And that's what I'm here to find out.'

'You'll find out more than you want to find out,' said Roderick. 'The police are on their trail.'

'Well, now!' said Woolly. 'I'm sorry about that.'

'It's too late to be sorry; you've probably led them up here. If that horse you're on belongs to that Fernandez fellow, it knows its way round a damn sight better than you do. You'd better go back while you can get back, and keep yourself out of other people's business.'

'You come back too,' invited Woolly.

'I'll come back when I want to,' said

Roderick. 'I know how to look after myself if it comes to a scrap, but I don't want you on my hands.'

'Well, now!' said Woolly mildly, once more. 'I—'

Whatever he was about to say was left unfinished. Two riders closed in on either side of Roderick. He felt stirrups, hard and sharp, pressing against his legs. The knees of the invisible riders pushed against his and forced him to move between them. No word was spoken, and the pace of the horses had not slackened, but Roderick knew that he and Woolly were being steered and he knew, with deadly certainty, what was pressing against his own ribs and what would happen if he made a sound.

There was a stir about them, and the escort closed in. Roderick felt himself pressed forward, and knew that they had joined a group of riders. Then he was brought to an abrupt halt, and he saw a single rider detach himself from the group and come towards them. The newcomer dismounted and Roderick and Woolly, obeying strong hints, did the same. Roderick found himself facing a tall, lean man, and while the keen eyes took him in, disordered hair, shredded coat and mangled trousers, Roderick made out strong features and an air of authority.

'English,' he said. 'Roderick Saracen.'

'You know who I am?' came a quiet voice.

'I can make a rough guess.'

'You and the señor followed me?'

'I can't answer for him, but I certainly didn't follow you.'

This was strictly true; he was not going to inform them that all the initiative came from the horse.

'You realize,' came the same polite, guarded voice, 'that neither of you can go back tonight?'

'Yes.'

'I will send you both with one of my men to a hut. You will be safe there. Tomorrow, he will take you both back to—'

The sentence remained unfinished. There was a whine and a thud, and a bullet passed no more than a foot over Roderick's head and buried itself in a near-by tree.

The next instant, the smugglers of Yago, in the province of Cádiz, were making for the shelter of the rocks. Leading them, leaping lightly over boulders, were Woolly Estwood and Roderick Saracen.

CHAPTER THIRTEEN

The battle began at dawn, but Woolly had no part in it. A prudent man and a peaceable man, he had decided that where bullets were, there would he not be. Roderick, he mused, was a war-like fellow, as he had always suspected. If he cared to stay ... Woolly, moving across in the darkness, ascertained that Roderick was certainly going to stay. For himself, if there was a hut where a man could sleep and be out of the way of bullets ...

There was no hut that could be reached with safety, but a lot could be done by a man who wanted to sleep in peace. There were rocky promontories. Woolly, feeling his way, selected the nearest natural shelter, crawled beneath it, stretched himself out and gave thanks that the night was not too chilly.

As the first rays of light appeared, Roderick was able to look about and study the company in which he found himself. He saw that there were eight men in the bare, rocky space in which they had spent the remaining hours of darkness. Don Manrique was the oldest, but only two of the party were youths; the others seemed to be between thirty and forty years of age, hardy, serious men, their dress and equipment picturesque enough, but reduced to a strict minimum for the business in hand. Roderick eyed their weapons and compared them with those he had seen carried by the Guardias Civiles the night before; there was nothing in it, he decided; if it came to real shooting, it would be a question of marksmanship. Both sides were, after all, Spaniards, and ought to be able to locate the bull's eye.

He had no hope that there would be a fight.

The stray bullet which had passed so unpleasantly close to him had been fired, he knew now, by one of the opposing force to indicate that he had been seen and followed. Don Manrique had no knowledge of the route by which he had come, and had judged it safer to wait for daylight before moving. The enemy might be behind them or round them; for the moment, they had natural and effective cover.

Roderick felt that the day would bring nothing but anticlimax. He had made a fool of himself; in fact, he had done worse: he had pushed his way into a fight which was none of his business, and he had ended up in the middle of those who were on what he considered to be the wrong side. Since he was here, since he had come so far and seen so much, he would have liked to see some real action, but he guessed that Don Manrique's plan was to find out where safety lay, and to seek it as rapidly as possible.

Roderick heard a low order from the leader, and saw two men crawl from shelter and vanish in the surrounding scrub. Two more went out of sight down the steep rock a few yards behind their hiding place. Don Manrique, immobile, expressionless, was training a pair of field-glasses on the hills in front of their position and Roderick, following the direction of his search, found himself gazing at a scene which drove from his mind, momentarily, the reason for his being privileged to feast his eyes upon it.

He was not, as a rule, moved by nature's beauties. He told himself, when he thought about it at all, that he knew scenery when he saw it, but, seeing it, did not feel himself disposed to become poetical. A view, after all, was merely a view. He had been in places high up on high hills where the view had been enough to take a man's breath away, but he had never found time to sit down and meditate upon it. He had stalked deer in Sctoland and tigers in India and lions in Kenya; the views had been magnificent—hill or plain, thicket or jungle—but all the thrills he had experienced had come from the chase and not from the back cloth.

But standing beside Don Manrique in the chill and stinging, clear and blood-stirring morning air, Roderick found himself studying his surroundings in a new mood. He had nothing to do; nobody was chasing him, and the danger—if danger there was—lay solely in the smugglers being rounded up and cast into prison to repent and to mend their ways. He was with them, but not of them. For the moment he was adrift; all he could do was wait until he could return—or be returned—to where he belonged. But in the meantime he could take his bearings and note that the view was something exceptional.

He found his mind darting here and there, collecting and annotating all that he had heard or read about the country which lay outspread at his feet. He could see, winding far, far below, a silver thread of river running like a child's wavering pencil mark across a brown page. Round the plain, on all sides, rose jagged and towering peaks. Men had stood where he was standing, and had looked down at Roman chariots and at Moors in flight; westward, he could see dimly the peaks which rose beyond the purple plains where great herds grazed, where the Andalusian bulls grow strong and know nothing of blood or sand or the shouts of the massed spectators round the bull ring. The herdsmen riding beside them wore the same costume which their ancestors had introduced across the Atlantic, and which was to become the pattern for the picturesque garb of the early American cowboy and later adopted by American children.

Roderick's eyes went back to the hills near by, and he knew that he was gazing at paths and passes over which centuries of Andalusian brigands had passed. Here, in country that would defeat the most experienced scout, bandits and smugglers had from time immemorable had their lairs. Here they moved swiftly over ground every foot of which they knew thoroughly; here they moved secretly by night until they were checked, as Don Manrique was checked now, by the unsportsmanlike interference of the law.

Don Manrique's scouts returned and reported to their leader, and Roderick, for the first time since coming to Spain, wished that he understood the language. He was beginning to feel useless; he was confident that he knew as much about catch-as-catch-can on steep mountainsides as any of these local players. It was galling to stand by and know that they considered him as a troublesome interloper, interfering, and very much in the way.

He saw presently that Don Manrique had decided to move. The horses, bunched together in a kind of cave a little way below, were being separated, and Roderick saw that the animal he had ridden the night before was being led apart from the others. For the first time since he had addressed him on his arrival, Don Manrique turned and spoke to Roderick.

'We are going on,' he said. 'One of my men will wait here until it is safe for you to go.' The stern expression relaxed for a moment. 'I am sorry that I was not able to see you when you came to my house.'

'Don't bother about escorts for me,' said Roderick shortly. 'I'll find my own way down.'

'It is not possible,' said Don Manrique. 'You will be stopped and questioned. One of my men will wait here. We are leaving now. Then he will take you back to—'

The word, Roderick thought afterwards, must have acted on each occasion as a signal. As in the darkness some hours earlier a bullet came from nowhere and ended the sentence in an unpleasant whine. And this time it was

200

followed by a fusillade that echoed among the hills and gave sufficient evidence that the enemy was awake and aware and in deadly earnest.

Real bullets!

Roderick's spirits soared with a speed that was only matched by the swiftness of his descent to cover. He saw the eight men round him taking careful aim; at a low word from Don Manrique, they opened fire.

Roderick looked cautiously about him. The marksmanship of the other side, he decided, was too accurate to be really safe. He had no idea how good his companions were, but they looked cool and competent and even a little contemptuous. He edged over to Don Manrique, and got a brief glance from the keen, dark eyes.

'Where?' asked Roderick, close by his side.

'There. Twelve.'

Twelve Guardias Civiles. Twelve black shiny Napoleonic hats behind those rocks on the hill below them. He had led them here, and it didn't matter whether he had meant to lead them or not; they were here and shooting. They were shooting to kill. This man beside him, who didn't want Nicholas to marry his daughter, was fighting his way out of a desperate situation. Smuggling, which had looked a low and sneaking business when contemplated from the armchair at the club, now assumed a dignity that roused in Roderick

201

a feeling amounting to something like respect. They carried cleaner cargo than he had supposed; they were only doing what tourists tried to do at every frontier, but they were doing it at a level of which Roderick thoroughly approved. They were doing it against odds, and they were playing for the highest stakes of all. Do or die. It was the creed of every right-thinking sportsman the world over. Lion, tiger, elephant—or Guardias Civiles. The hunt was on, and he stood here—a spectator, weaponless, useless, ridiculous, and redundant.

'No more rifles?' he asked Don Manrique.

The dark eyes rested on him for a moment in surprise, in speculation, and then in a kind of reluctant amusement.

'No.'

'I'm a pretty average shot.'

'Please. You will keep away.'

He kept away. The men round him shot, reloaded, sighted—and Roderick looked on.

In time, they found themselves giving ground. They made their way, by spurts, to a space that offered less cover but more opportunity for manoeuvre. They had separated, and Roderick, returning on his stomach from a one-man reconnoitring patrol, felt himself more in touch with the plan of battle. He crept cautiously to a point at which he was close to Don Manrique, and spoke to him across the intervening scrub.

'Four of them—in a pocket,' he said. 'Tell a couple of your men off; two'll be enough to take care of them.'

'Please do not interfere.' There was no coldness in the request, it was merely a plea; it meant that Don Manrique considered he had enough on his hands without the addition of a dead Englishman.

'Give me two men,' requested Roderick. 'I'd like those two thugs over ... those two big ones over there.'

'Take them,' said Don Manrique.

Roderick took them. The pocket became too hot, and the enemy found it expedient to leave it and move to a cooler retreat.

'Told you so,' reported Roderick, on his return. 'You ought to—'

'I have been fighting the Guardias Civiles,' said Don Manrique, 'for thirty years.'

'Quite so. If I could take that fellow over there and—'

There was a sudden and confused interruption. The smack of a bullet on a near-by rock was followed by a grunt from the young man firing on Roderick's left. There was the clatter of a rifle falling to the ground and Roderick saw the man's hand go to his shoulder, and knew that the right arm was hanging uselessly. Before anyone had done more than register the sounds, Roderick had leaned forward and picked up the rifle.

'No,' said Don Manrique.

'Not bad,' commented Roderick, stroking his weapon.

'You will please—'

'For God's sake,' said Roderick, in a burst of irritation, 'will you mind your own blasted business?'

The cavalcade moved by night, not because there was any more fear of the enemy, for the enemy had been scattered and had retreated to regroup, or to reinforce, or to reconsider. There was no more fear from them, but secrecy was still desirable ... necessary. Not for the contraband, for that was safe. That was in good hands, and when the horses reached the next rendezvous, far up there in the remote hills, it would pass into equally safe keeping for the next stage of its journey. The cargo was safe; it only remained to convey the wounded in secret to their homes. Two wounded; Paco, whose shoulder had been skilfully bound and who was lying in his home beyond Yago. And the Englishman. It was essential, it was above all things necessary to get the Englishman back with speed and secrecy, before the news of his wound spread and reached those who would insist upon holding an enquiry.

And so the small cavalcade came down the steep slopes; in front, Tio Pepe, who had not been in the fight, but who had been fetched so that the number continuing the journey should not be further depleted. After him, the Englishman on a stretcher slung between two mules; after him, Don Manrique, who wished to accompany his comrade in arms; bringing up the rear, the second Englishman, who had shown a total lack of interest in the battle and concerned himself only with seeing that no harm came to the horses.

They came by strange paths, and kept far away from the roads. Only when the lights gleamed below them, when the Casa de Nuestra Señora del Carmen was before them, did they venture where other men passed, and make their way to the great door.

The door stood open. Word had gone before them, sent by Don Manrique, and had reached his daughter, and she took it to Lorna in her sitting-room, where the four of them— Carmela, Lorna, Nicholas and Martin—had waited through a night and a day and part of another night.

'The Señor is wounded,' said Carmela quietly. 'They are bringing him home.'

*   *   *

Roderick opened his eyes to find himself in a strange bed in a strange room. He knew that he was bandaged, but he felt no pain; only a slight discomfort and a great sense of achievement. The eyes which met Lorna's had lost none of their cool and confident light; they rested upon her as she stood at the foot of the bed, and took in her pallor and her droop of fatigue.

'We licked 'em,' he said.

'How do you feel, Roderick?'

'Average. What's the damage?'

'The shot went through cleanly, just below the shoulder. The leg is the trouble; they think it might be more than a sprain.'

'Nonsense. If the damned stones hadn't slipped, I'd have been all right. I couldn't have fallen more than a few feet.'

'You feel fifteen feet, and rolled another twenty. You ought to have been killed.'

'Nonsense.'

'What, in heaven's name, made you do such a thing?'

'Couldn't say,' the question reassured him. That Woolly fellow had obviously kept his own counsel; he doubted, indeed, whether anybody knew of his part in the affair. He was not, he decided firmly, going to say a word more than he needed to on the subject; the circumstances leading up to his exploit would remain for ever a secret between himself and the horse.

'How did the dinner-party go?' he enquired.

Lorna sat on the end of the bed and looked at him from under puzzled brows.

'Aren't you going to explain?' she asked.

'There's nothing to explain. I wanted to see how those smuggling chaps went on, and I saw, that's all. I don't say I actually intended to get mixed up in anything, but the odds seemed to be against them.'

'Don't pretend you thought of the odds. You smelt powder and shot and you didn't think at all; you just joined in. You gave us a lot of worry.'

'Did you know where I was?'

'We could guess. We could conjecture, but it didn't make sense. The boys wanted to go after you. And Carmela—'

She fell silent, thinking of Carmela. She had wondered, at times, how much the girl knew of her father's intermittent and unlawful excursions, but now she wondered no longer. From the moment the servants, on that night which now seemed so far away, had reported the arrival of Roderick in the car and his inexplicable departure on the horse, Carmela had shown a calm and clear knowledge of what was likely to take place. She had been able to assess the consequences of Roderick's action, and outlined them to Nicholas and Martin. There had been nothing to do but wait; he would come back, or he would be brought back.

'How long have I been here?' enquired Roderick.

'I invited you to dinner on Thursday— Martin's birthday. You disappeared that night. This is Saturday morning; Don Manrique brought you back by night and you got here at three o'clock this morning. The doctor—my doctor—came at five. It's now eleven.'

207

'I'm damned hungry.'

'I suppose you are,' said Lorna.

'Has there been any enquiry about me from Gib?'

'No. When the servants told me about your—your extraordinary behaviour, I rang up Gibraltar and said that you would be here for the night. I rang up next day and said you were staying on, and they sent over your things.'

'Good. We don't want anybody poking their noses in and making unnecessary trouble. Hadn't you better see about a meal for me?'

'The doctor said nothing about meals.'

'I don't care for any of those Spanish dishes with fried stuff in them. Steak, if you've got any in the house. Don't let them overdo it; I like a touch of red left in it. Potatoes in their jackets, and a decent bit of cheese to finish up with. Not goat cheese; cow cheese. I could drink something, too. Something in the claret line.'

'With a bullet wound?'

'With the steak,' said Roderick.

She rose and stood looking at him, and he looked back at her with speculation and something else in his glance.

'You used to be a rotten nurse,' he said. 'You nursed me through that go of flu, and put my recovery back by several days.'

'And I caught it from you.'

'Yes. Nemesis. Do I get that food, or do I have to shout and attract the attention of half a

208

dozen of the staff?'

'I'll order something for you.'

The door closed behind her and did not open again for some time. Roderick wondered, with some annoyance, why his sons did not come in to see him. They must be somewhere about, and they ought to be able to spare a moment to look in and ask him how he was.

There was a discreet scratch at the door, and it opened to admit a manservant carrying an apparatus which Roderick recognized as a bed table of the sensible type that could be swivelled in front of the patient. With a grunt of satisfaction he allowed another servant to prop him up on his pillows while a third wheeled in a neat trolley on which was a covered dish. From the dish came a smell that made the patient's mouth water. A tray with a fresh white cloth and gleaming silver was laid before him and a dish laid upon it. The dishcover was taken off, and Roderick found himself looking at a thin, nourishing soup.

It smelt all right, he mused, taking up a spoon. Something to start off with, though he never cared for soup with his meals. The steak would follow.

Nothing followed. The empty dish was removed and so, to the horror of the patient, was the fresh white cloth, the gleaming silver and the tray. The bed table swung away and the trolley was wheeled away and the servants—

'Hey!' called Roderick.

'Señor?'

'I said steak.'

'Señor?'

'Don't stand there. Fetch somebody who can do something. Go and get me a—'

He stopped. A girl was standing in the open doorway, and he had no difficulty in guessing who she was—small and dark-haired and with eyes that rested on him with the same calm gaze as those other eyes had done up there in the mountains.

'You're Carmela,' he stated.

'Yes.'

'Well, look here, Carmela; I ordered food, and I didn't get it.'

She was in the room; the servants had retired and closed the door behind them.

'You will eat in good time,' she said.

'The only good time for eating is when a man's hungry. I'm not peckish, I'm wolfish. I told my—I told Lorna—'

'She ordered soup.'

'Well, would you very kindly go and tell her I—'

'I am here,' said Carmela, 'to nurse you.'

'*Nurse* me?'

'Yes.'

'Nonsense.'

'Somebody must nurse you, and we cannot ask somebody from outside. We do not want anybody to know about anything. I am a very good nurse.'

'Where's Nicholas,' demanded Roderick.

'He was coming to see you, and so was Martin. But when they heard that you wanted steak and would not get steak, they said that they would come and see you some other time.'

'Do you mean to tell me I'm going to lie here like a dummy and—'

'There are bandages to be changed. There are medicines to be given. I can reassure you that I am competent.'

She looked it. In spite of her small frame and soft beauty, she looked extremely competent as she stood there looking at him, her childish mouth firm and determined, and her eyes—his heart sank—clear and unafraid.

'Where's your father?' he asked presently.

'He came here with you. Now he has gone back to Yago; he thought it would be wiser, in case there was talk ... rumours. He will come again.'

Back to Yago. It was over. The night and the battle and the sweet sense of danger. Men had gone out to hunt men; there had been a quickening of his blood and he had fallen in with the hunted in the closest companionship of all—the comradeship of men who risked their lives together. There had been speed and action; there had been a thrill of pure triumph when he had made a hole straight through one of the corners of a black, shiny hat.

It was over.

'Pity,' remarked Roderick, to nobody in particular.

CHAPTER FOURTEEN

Roderick would rather have found himself anywhere but at the Casa del Carmen, but he was as anxious to keep the details of his recent exploit from spreading as Don Manrique could be, and he understood the latter's wisdom in bringing him to the house. He went on to acknowledge to himself that if he had to be laid up anywhere, he could have chosen no more comfortable place for his convalescence than this pleasant bedroom opening on to a wide, vine-shaded verandah. His early mistrust of Carmela as a nurse had faded; she was cool, impersonal and efficient, and he had learned that her soft, red lips could close firmly and that her large eyes could meet his with steady purpose shining in them. While he was in bed, he was forced to submit to her dictums; then he graduated to a long chair on the verandah, and from that moment began to regain his lost initiative, and was soon in a position to get his own way in everything except the matter of diet. Until he was to find his way to the kitchens and hold up the staff at pistol-point until they understood that a big man must be fed, he would have to exercise patience.

He found little to ruffle the smooth surface of his existence. While Carmela was his nurse, there was a tacit agreement between them to avoid the topic of her marriage to Nicholas; the latter had returned to Gibraltar, but came to the Casa del Carmen whenever he could, and spent most of his visits in his father's room. Martin was in and out of the room all day; Lorna paid a visit every morning, and returned whenever he sent for her. He had given orders to Carmela to exclude all other visitors but Woolly. Stephanie had got in once, nobody knew how, but Roderick had met the situation by falling instantly into a deep coma which lasted until the visitor went away.

Woolly did not come. Roderick wondered a little, but was content to wait. Reedy, melancholy sounds sometimes came from the direction of the waggon and Roderick sent out a strong message to the effect that the noise disturbed him. Woolly as a man who, in certain matters, believed that honesty was only a second-best policy replied that he wasn't making it, and went on making it.

Life at the Casa del Carmen seemed to have settled down to most of its former restfulness, but there were signs that Roderick's presence had caused more than a temporary disturbance. Florence was the person most affected, and she spoke her feelings to Lorna at the first opportunity.

'Lorna,' she asked abruptly, 'would you like

me to go?'

Lorna stared at her.

'Go? You mean go away?'

'Yes.'

'Why should I want you to? I like having you here. Do you want to go anywhere special?'

'I don't want to go away at all,' declared Florence. 'I don't mean that I've settled here for life, but I hadn't really planned to leave for a month or two. But—'

'Well, what?'

'Whenever I happen to pass the verandah— and I have to pass it sometimes, you know, on my way down to Woolly's—I can feel two eyes boring holes right through my back.'

'Does that worry you?' enquired Lorna.

'That's neither here nor there. What I meant was, that he won't be chained up there for much longer, and when he gets into the body of the house, he'll be everywhere. There won't be any place I can go to be out of the way of that look, and I can't spend my entire life shut away in my own rooms, can I?'

'Aren't you exaggerating his importance a little?'

'All I'm saying is that it'll be like having a grizzly bear walking about loose. It might hurt me, or it mightn't, but I just don't care to find out, that's all.'

'You're surely not frightened of Roderick?'

'That's what I asked Woolly, and Woolly spoke up like a man and said he was scared

214

stiff. Well, I won't say I'm scared, but if he looks at me straight in the eye with that look, then don't expect me to look straight back. I'd go away and think nothing of it and come back when he's gone, but then I say to myself, how can I go away and leave you alone with him and nobody to hold him off?'

'Florence, you don't imagine that I can't manage Roderick, surely?'

'Well, can you?'

'What do you think he's going to do with me?'

'Well, he's pretty comfortable, and he must know it. What's to stop him from making up his mind to make his home here?'

'Nothing would ever induce him to.'

'All right; you know him better than I do. I'm only judging by his appearance, but that's dangerous enough, goodness knows. I've got a strong feeling I want to stay here and look out for you.'

'You're sweet, and I hope you'll stay, but I don't want anybody to look after me, thank you.'

'And there's another thing. Martin used to be down there with Woolly, day after day, talking to him. Now he only goes down once in a while, and when he does go, he doesn't talk about his gardens.'

'I think I know why. He feels that his father is—'

'I know what you're going to say. His
215

father's out of the way for the moment, and so it isn't whatsit … cricket to go fixing anything behind his back. Well, I say that this is our last chance, and we ought to go ahead and fix it all up before he gets a chance to get out and spoil everything.'

'I don't think Martin would—'

'I've just been telling you, Martin won't. Just because his father falls off a horse. What was he doing, riding in the first place, Lorna? What got into you, to ask him to stay the night?'

'Well, I—'

'If you hadn't asked him, he wouldn't have been here the next day to go for a ride, and then this wouldn't have happened.'

'No.'

There had been, unfortunately, a little confusion over the details of the story given out to explain Roderick's accident. There had been a hurried decision to keep the night's work a secret as far as possible, and Nicholas had told his mother that he would 'concoct something,' and had built up what he felt to be a hole-proof explanation of his father's accident. The account he had given Florence had been convincing enough, but there had been no time to ensure that the others would tell the same story. Pressed for details, Lorna and Martin did their best, but there accounts were somewhat confused, and there were now as many conflicting versions as those of eye-witnesses after an accident.

Woolly's instinct was, like Florence's, to work fast and seal matters before Roderick had the opportunity of interfering, but nothing could be done without Martin, and Martin could seldom be reached; he was with his father for most of the day, playing chess with him, or piquet, or making a fourth at bridge with Nicholas and Lorna. He came down and listened to Woolly's music, but met appeals to talk business with the plea that his father was unable, as yet, to take part in the discussions. Woolly had made up his mind that as soon as Roderick felt able to take part, he himself would think of something that would take him a long and safe distance from the Casa del Carmen, but he found it difficult to explain this satisfactorily to Martin without explaining that he had taken a more active part in Roderick's exploit than had been popularly supposed. He was uncertain what his part had been, but he remembered that Roderick had accused him of leading the police up the mountainside. And they were police bullets that had winged him. As soon as Roderick was about again, he would go away; he explained this clearly to his sister.

'Then you're running out on me?' asked Florence.

'Yes,' said Woolly.

But it was too late to run.

Roderick was up, and was walking to and fro on the verandah—and enjoying it. A slight limp, he acknowledged, but that would soon go. A slight stiffness here and there, but on the whole, he'd mended. He was whole. He was free.

He heard a light footstep and turned. Carmela had come out onto the verandah and was watching him. Without speaking, he walked to and fro several times more, and she nodded gravely.

'Yes,' she said.

'Nice to be about again,' commented Roderick.

'I am glad for you,' said Carmela.

'Sit down,' he said.

She walked to the verandah steps and sat on the topmost one and looked up at him quietly.

'You're not a bad nurse,' he said.

'Thank you.'

'Not at all. Thank *you*.'

There was a pause, but it was merely a pause to enable Roderick to choose the right words. He had had a good deal of time to think; there had been no opportunity for anything else but thinking, but now was the time for action. He knew what he wanted, and it was time other people knew, too. Half the trouble in the world, he considered, was caused by people who couldn't find out the truth for themselves, and wouldn't believe it when it was pointed out to them. Think clearly; act promptly. If there was a better maxim for a man, he couldn't, at this moment, think of one.

'I suppose,' he said, 'that you and Nicholas think I'm being unreasonable?'

'Yes, but my father is being unreasonable, too,' said Carmela in generous excuse.

'Then that makes two of us; two people of experience, with our heads well screwed on our shoulders. Doesn't that look as though we might be right?'

'In a way you are both right,' said Carmela calmy. 'It would have been more convenient if I had fallen in love with my cousin, but I did not.'

'Do you think you'll be happy away from'—Roderick waved a hand—'all this?'

'With Nicholas, yes.'

'Wives of naval men don't have much of a time, on the whole.'

'When their husbands are away, they have their children.'

'My feeling is,' said Roderick, whose feeling was that they were not making headway, 'that you should put it all away in cold storage for a year.'

'in—?'

'I think that Nicholas should go away and that you should both think it over for a year. A year isn't much out of your lives, if it's going to prevent you from making a mess of the rest of them. Don't see one another for a year; at the end of that time, if you're both of the same mind and still keen on the engagement, I promise to withdraw my objections. That's fair enough, isn't it?'

'It sounds fair,' said Carmela, in the tone of one reasoning with an argumentative child. 'It sounds very fair.'

'But you won't do it?'

'I shall ask Nicholas.'

That was a good enough start; if he saw Nicholas before she did, he could put the case more strongly. The girl didn't seem to have taken it in fully, but she'd got the hang of it. She was a pretty enough little thing, and it was easy to see what had got into the boy, but there must be something more than big black eyes and one of those bunchy little mouths and a capacity for good nursing. If they could be got away from one another and allowed to cool off, a lot might happen. She'd probably find that a handsome Spaniard would suit her a good deal better, and Nicholas could settle down with a girl who could stand child-bearing and a northern climate. There was no question of acting the heavy parent; a quiet word of sense and an appeal to their judgment. He felt that he had done the thing well; when Lorna came in, he would talk to her about it.

Lorna heard him as calmly as Carmela had done.

'What did she say?' she asked, at the end of his recital.

'Said she'd put it to Nicholas. She's a pliable enough type; if I can make him see sense, I can make her see it without much trouble. I'm

220

feeling rather hopeful about the whole thing.'

'I'm glad,' said Lorna.

He looked across at her. Like Carmela, she was listening to him on the verandah, but she was not sitting on the step; she was on a long, low chair and she looked relaxed and rather lazy and not at all, he felt with some irritation, like a woman who was discussing a crisis in her son's life.

'You don't agree with any of it, of course,' he said stiffly.

'No,' said Lorna, 'but I'm sure you won't let that worry you.'

'You're trying to make me look like the Barretts of Wimpole Street,' he said resentfully, 'but it strikes me that you're only concerned with the romantic aspect of this attachment. I'm thinking of their future.'

'And trying to make certain that they won't have one together.'

'Are you going to side against me,' he demanded.

'I'm not going to open a campaign; I shall simply give them my blessing and hope they'll have enough sense to get married in spite of you.'

'It doesn't strike you, does it, that I've more say in my son's affairs than you have?'

'I've told you, Roderick, you're suffering from the difficulty that all parents experience when their children become men and women; you just don't realize it. You're treating

Nicholas as though he were a boy of about seventeen. I suppose I'd make the same mistake too, if I'd seen him growing up, but I saw him first as a completely adult person, calling on me to talk to me about the woman he wanted to make his wife. If you and Don Manrique had got together and worked on the problem, instead of playing smugglers up there, we shouldn't have had a problem at all.'

'Well, I think I've solved it. Don't go, there was something else.'

Lorna sat back once more and prepared to listen.

'I've been watching that woman,' began Roderick, 'and I think you ought to talk to her and induce her to pack up and go.'

'Which woman?'

'You know quite well. The painted one.'

'Florence is a friend of mine.'

'Then she shouldn't be; she's not at all your type, and I can't understand how you ever came to tolerate her. How did she came to be here so long? Has she settled down for ever? Where's her husband? Where does all that money of hers come from? Why hasn't she got a home of her own?'

'I'm not going to answer any of those questions, because it's simply none of your business.'

'Certainly it isn't but when you've lived with a woman, when you've been man and wife and when you meet again, you feel a normal,

222

friendly interest in her affairs. I know you, don't forget. I know that anybody with a plausible yarn could always get round you. My God, don't I remember having old Aunt Thornycroft on our hands for a whole winter because you thought her house wasn't warm enough for a woman with a weak chest? You're what they call nowadays a soft touch, Lorna, and this woman knows it. If she can afford to buy a house of her own, then encourage her to go away and buy one. If you drift any more, you'll have her digging herself in like one of those royal pensioners. I daresay she might have been company for you, of a sort, but good God! you don't have to house her for ever! This whole place is crawling with odds and ends of people, most of them on the payroll.'

'I do wish you'd understand, Roderick, that it isn't anything to do with you.'

'I hate to see you robbed, that's all. Money is money. Do you really need four people to wait at table?'

'Wages here are very low.'

'Wages are the least of it. You feed them, don't you? And every one of them eats their head off. If you must employ them, do you have to employ their wives and daughters, too?'

'We're all extremely happy here.'

'Who the devil's talking of happiness? I'm talking about money. You haven't changed, you know. I can remember raising your dress allowance, and you went out with the children and came back with a crate of hopelessly unsuitable toys. Who in God's name wanted a Punch and Judy show?'

'I did,' said Lorna.

'That's what you said at the time, I remember.'

'I remember what you said, too.'

'I suppose you do. You've got a long memory for anything you can hold against a man.'

He sat in silence, brooding over his wrongs, and then pulled himself back to the present.

'That girl,' he said. 'That so-called secretary of yours.'

'Well, I'll admit that she's rather a trial.'

'Isn't she Portalloway's daughter?'

'Yes. She's the only child.'

'Damn shame. He doesn't deserve it. His wife was a nice enough woman, too. As far as I can see, there's nothing in either of them to account for this Viceroy Sarah they've produced. Why haven't you done anything about getting rid of her?'

'She's engaged to somebody who's gone away for a time.'

'If she's engaged, and if he's gone away for a time, he's obviously going to stay away, and I'm not going to blame him. That girl doesn't need a husband, or children either. She's missed her vocation. She ought to be one of those professional guides who walk round followed by a flock of docile tourists, pouring facts and dates into them. That's not a bad idea, as a matter of fact; I think I could get her fixed up with one of those firms in Gibraltar, she could deal with all those boatloads of Americans they keep putting ashore there. She could march 'em up and down the Rock, giving out information; it won't do much in the way of making them love the British, but a lot of them don't, anyway. I've got some pull; I'll fix it up as soon as I get back there. It'll be better than sending her home and saddling poor old Portalloway and his wife with her. I'll write to Portalloway and tell him what I'm doing. I owe him a good turn; he got me those fishing rights last year up in Scotland. Funny ... I didn't dream, then, that I'd be sitting with you now, discussing his daughter.'

He sat silent for some time. Lorna, who had listened to his summary disposal of her secretary with secret gratitude, saw a soft gleam of reminiscence beginning to shine in his eye, and hastened into speech.

'Do you feel well enough to have lunch with us?' she asked him. 'Some people are coming over; you know them, I think. There's—'

'That Freeman fellow, I suppose?'

'Yes. And—'

'He practically lives here. You don't get much work out of these chaps nowadays. I don't know what the naval rates of pay are at the moment, but I know one or two who don't do much except smooch off and leave the job to somebody else. The only time they're on hand is when it's time to grab their pay packets.'

'About lunch—?'

'Thank you. I'll have mine here,' said Roderick.

Lorna rose, and his eyes rested on her and took in the lovely lines of her body and the easy grace of her movements. He had held her, he remembered disturbingly, in his arms. He had imprisoned that warm flesh ... once, long ago. His hands, his lips, his body remembered her. She was the mother of his children. They had met and loved, passionately, and she had belonged to him. His demands had been fierce and her responses ardent. Even if they had both forgotten, Nicholas and Martin remained to recall those years. But he had not forgotten. Rising to his feet and standing before her, Roderick realized that he was remembering a great deal too much. But the eyes into which he had looked once with love and longing, were looking into his now with a calm politeness that one stranger would show to another. They were strangers, he and she, and she was walking away down the steps and into the bright garden, and soon she would be smiling with warmth and eagerness at other men, while he sat here alone and remembered the past.

'Lorna!' he called.

She glanced back fleetingly and hastened her steps.

226

She was gone. Roderick was left to sit there alone and remember the past.

CHAPTER FIFTEEN

Woolly was totally unprepared. He had maintained a strict watch and had ascertained, from his vantage point in the undergrowth, that two cars, gleaming and beflagged and bearing a Gibraltar number-plate, stood outside the house; on the verandah, extra chairs had been placed and distinguished figures sat upon them. Putting all these things together, Woolly had brooded upon them for some time and had then drawn a reassuring conclusion: visitors, big shots, from the Rock.

With a sigh of relief, he had felt it safe to relax for a time, and he had got out his most comfortable chair and put his feet up and covered his head with a handkerchief and closed his eyes and rejoiced in his little patch of sunshine. But the visits were over in less time than that which was understood, among Woolly's friends, to be the correct for social calls, and thus it came about that a large form threw a shadow over the chair and Woolly sat up with a jerk and heard a voice informing him that it was a nice place he'd got there.

'Ah,' said Woolly.

Roderick found a chair and sat on it.

227

'Nice to be about again,' he said.

'Ah,' said Woolly.

'I had no idea your—er—outfit was as large as this. I imagined it was a sort of caravan, but I see it's more like a camp. Very ingenious.'

'Ah.'

'You've got a fine view of the water from here.'

'Ah.'

'Pleasant weather, on the whole.'

'Ah.' There was a pause. 'Glad you feel better,' said Woolly.

'Thanks.'

'You shouldn't have gone chasing smugglers. I could have told you it wasn't a safe thing to do. Want to look round the place?'

Roderick felt no wish to look round, but there was an undercurrent of wistfulness in the question that moved him before he could put up any resistance. He found himself agreeing, and the next moment Woolly had led him out of the tent and was showing him the mysteries of his mobile home. The man in Roderick became submerged, after a time, to the small boy; he had not seen anything like this, he told Woolly, since he laid out his sons' Combined Forces on the floor of the nursery. His opinion of his host rose every moment; the fellow, he told himself with a touch of self-reproach, wasn't the nitwit he appeared to be. Far from it. He was a hairless wonder; there had been

228

nothing like this for ingenuity since Robinson's day, Crusoe or Swiss Family.

'Wait a minute,' said Woolly, now completely absorbed and happy. 'I'll fix up that observation platform and—'

'I suppose you know what I weigh?'

'It'll hold you, all except the top storey. I reckon I can see a lot of miles when I get right up there.'

'It's giving you a lot of trouble.'

'Pleasure, more like it. Gives me a kick to have people come out and look the place over.'

'Want a hand?'

'No, no, I've got everything fixed so's I can manage without a crew. Stand aside now while I swing this up—that's the way it goes. Now it's lifting—see? Now you can go up—steady now. Don't you go beyond that second platform.'

One of the laundry maids in the servants' quarters, chancing to look up from her work of hanging out the clothes, gave a wild shriek of terror and tried to explain to her startled fellow workers that something in human form had appeared above the trees, turned slowly on its base, and vanished. Straining their eyes, they looked in the direction she indicated, and saw nothing, but there could not be any doubt, from the girl's deadly pallor, that there had been something. Work was suspended while they walked to the village to put the matter before El Cura.

'Saw for miles,' said Roderick, letting

229

himself down carefully on his good leg. 'Bally marvel. Got any more gadgets?'

Woolly had several more, but the one of which he was most proud was his shower bath.

'Never had one before,' he explained to Roderick. 'Used to have a bath now'n again, but it took time—kind of clumsy. This way I can pump the water from the sea up to that canvas tank up there, and—well, come and I'll show you.'

They walked a few yards and came round the side of a small tent.

'I suppose you put it here,' said Roderick, 'because—'

He came to a dead stop, his mouth open. Woolly, by his side, followed the direction of his gaze and felt his new-found confidence oozing steadily out of him. There was a dead silence as the two men stared straight before them.

'Good ... Lord,' said Roderick at last, on a long breath.

He had walked out of a setting of cork, lemon, orange and eucalyptus trees straight to the borders of an old English flower garden. He was staring at begonias and antirrhinums, at dahlias and petunias and pink geraniums and delphiniums. They swung him, with a wrenching shock, from his present surroundings to the familiar, loved forms and colours of his garden at home. He forgot, for an instant, the Casa del Carmen, its spreading grounds and their lavish colour and brilliance; he was for one sweet moment where he belonged.

'I didn't mean for you to see those,' mumbled Woolly. 'I just forget I'd put 'em all out there.'

Roderick had recovered. His glance at the flowers was now keen and critical, and his first pleasure was being rapidly succeeded by distaste.

'Martin's,' he said.

'Yes. I've had them out there a long time, seeing how much they could stand in the way of sun and sea-water and a bit of rough treatment. They stand up fine.'

'Those were what I came to see you about.'

'Yes. Well, I guess you've got to talk about it. I'd like to show you the rest of my fixings first, though.'

'Later,' said Roderick. 'My leg could do with a rest.'

'Myself,' said Woolly, when they were settled, 'I think the boy's idea is good.'

'I'm afraid I don't agree with you.'

'When you saw those flowers just now, out there, they had you fooled for a moment, didn't they.'

'I'll admit they did.'

'And they made you feel good.'

'Briefly, I suppose. But to know that they were nothing but fakes—'

'Nobody,' said Woolly, going to what he felt
231

was the heart of the matter, 'is going to ask you for any money.'

'This isn't a question of money. I'd put my son into business if I felt that the business had a future. But nothing could ever come of this. It's fantastic. In fact, I'll go further and say that I think there's something indecent in the idea of people wanting an array of artificial flowers on show round their houses. The idea sickens me.'

'I've told Martin that it won't go in England.'

'Certainly it won't. Or anywhere else. And I think when Martin's a bit older, he'll be damn glad his name hasn't been associated with a scheme of this kind. It's been an interesting hobby for him, but it oughtn't to be allowed to interfere with his future.'

'Even if you didn't believe in it, someone else might.'

'Nobody with any pretensions to good taste or good feeling could consider it. The boy would be a laughing stock.'

'A lot of pretty good ideas have been laughed at.'

'You're very kind,' said Roderick, and meant it. 'But you're not an Englishman, and so you'll have to take my word for this: if you try to market anything of the kind in England, you'll be howled down.'

'That's what I'm trying to tell you. But I've got friends in the building trade where I come from; I worked with them once, and I'd like to

232

get hold of one of them and ask him to let me put up a sample garden next time he puts up a house. Where's the harm in that?'

'You'd be wasting your time and your money.'

Woolly would have liked to point out that he had plenty of both, and should be allowed to do what he liked with his own. But he had done his best to marshal his ideas and place them before Roderick, and he saw no evidence that he had made any impression.

'I said my piece,' he explained to his sister later, 'and it didn't do any good.'

'Why didn't you tell him he wasn't doing the best he could for his son,' demanded Florence.

'Well, because he thinks he is, Flo.'

'You couldn't have talked strongly to him.'

'Yes, I did, but he kept making objections, and they were the same objections, but he made 'em sound different each time. You don't get on when you talk to him, Flo; you only go round and round.'

'Well, it isn't for him to decide,' summed up Florence. 'It's for Martin. We'll just have to wait and see what Martin decides, that's all.'

Not far away Nicholas was struggling to make a decision of his own.

He had driven over from Gibraltar, and he had hesitated at the cross-road leading up to Yago. He could go up and see Carmela, or he could go on to the Casa del Carmen and talk it over with his mother.

233

On reflection, he decided to do neither of these things. This was a matter for himself only; he'd played round it too long, and he was going to come to grips with it now—at once—and make his decision. And he would stick to it. He would worry it out alone, here. Better still, he'd go along to the village and get hold of Domingo and get him to take him out for a bit of fishing; it would be quiet, and he could think.

He turned the car and drove into Estronella and took the sandy lane that led down to the fishermen's cottages. he parked the car somewhat precariously on a stony slope, and getting out, made his way to the battered white cottage in which Domingo and his family lived. There was no sign of Domingo, but there were several small girls standing by who looked as though they might know where he was. After waiting for a few minutes, Nicholas raised his eyebrows enquiringly and pointed vaguely and then spread out his hands in what he felt to be a typically Spanish gesture.

'Domingo?' he enquired.

'Si, si, si! Si, si!' yelled a chorus of voices. There was a concerted rush to the house at the end of the row. The messengers vanished inside and reappeared shortly with a short, sleepy-looking man who wore a dark blue beret tilted over one eye, at such an angle that one wondered what kept it from slipping off. He came up to Nicholas, and by a process of

234

voluble outcries on the part of Domingo and explanatory additions from the chorus, filled out with some energetic pantomime from Nicholas, the arrangement was made; the boat would be got ready. Immediately.

Nicholas was sufficiently familiar with the Spanish notion of time to understand what immediately meant. He propped himself up against a wall, lit a cigarette and gave himself up to patient waiting. There was no hurry, and there was plenty to look at.

The small girls sat in a circle round him, and Nicholas saw that many of them were in the almost inevitable mourning. It was this Spanish habit of having relatives, he mused; naturally, they were always dying off, leaving the survivors swathed in heavy black. It worked out, roughly, at two or three years when papa or mamma passed on or popped off; a mere six months for granny or granpa, and a contemptuous three months or so for uncle and auntie. It was odd to look at that eleven-year-old sitting there making eyes at him and to see her in a long-sleeved black dress in this sunny and colourful setting. Perhaps that was the reason they all went in for all those blazing colours in the short intervals between the mourning periods.

Two little boys joined the spectators; Domingo strolled to and from the boat, making ready in leisurely fashion. Some time later, the boat was in the water and the gear

235

was aboard; the fisherman was at the oars and they were ready to go.

Nicholas rolled up his trousers and listened to the sudden shrill outcries of the small boys and girls. Domingo, pausing, raised a hand to still the clamour and looked across at Nicholas, speaking several sentences in a rapid and unintelligible flow. Nicholas gave a shrug of non-comprehension and Domingo, leaning forward and raising his voice as though addressing the deaf, repeated his previous statement.

'You chaps all gabble too much,' said Nicholas. 'If you'd go at it slowly, there might be a chance of someone's picking up one word in every ten, but while you just sit there and go *purraburrapurraburra* at me, the whole thing's pretty hopeless.'

'No?' said Domingo, disappointed.

'Oh, by all means,' said Nicholas. 'Whatever it was. Yes. Si, si, si.'

The result appalled him. With a wild scream of delight every one of the children standing, half-submerged, on the beach, began to clamber into the boat. As the vessel rocked from side to side, the swarm, screaming, came aboard. They sat where they could; those who could not find seats crouched at the feet of Nicholas and Domingo. The two boys, attempting to follow, were beaten off by the girls, and, shouting, swam for some distance behind the boat. Through the clamour,

236

Nicholas looked across at Domingo, and understood, from his gestures, that they were bound for a small beach a few hundred yards away. This was not, for the moment, a fishing expedition; it was a joy ride. The children, who could have walked to the beach in less time than it would take Domingo to row them there, were being given a treat.

They reached the beach, but before they disembarked, the children undressed. Black cotton frocks were pulled off; white cotton petticoats followed and revealed a simple bathing costume of a pair of cotton knickers. The two youngest maidens divested themselves of these, and gave them to Nicholas to hold; then the screaming began afresh as brown figure after brown figure scrambled over the side of the boat and waded to the shore. Domingo waited until all the swimmers were ashore and then, rolling up their garments into one indiscriminate heap, flung it after them. The excited shrieks died away; the white houses of the village receded; Nicholas looked over the side of the boat and stared at the still water, deep and deeper.

He had meant to wrestle with his problem, to look at it from all sides, to sift, to weigh. He had meant to put himself in the place of everybody concerned, and argue from their standpoint. He had meant ... But when they returned, and the boat touched the shore once more, when Domingo steadied the boat and

Nicholas set foot on the beach, he realized that he had not done any of the things he had meant to do. He had put the problem aside and had thought of nothing but the things of the moment.

Nevertheless, as he got into his car and backed it away from the slope and turned, he knew that his decision was made. Where or how, he could not have told, but he knew, with certainty, what he meant to do. It only remained now to go to Yago and tell Carmela.

Driving round the familiar curves, swinging round the hairpin bends, he knew that the struggles of the past weeks were over. He felt at peace and at ease.

Presently, he broke into song.

CHAPTER SIXTEEN

'It's time I went,' said Roderick.

Lorna wanted to agree with him, but she kept silent. Carmela had gone long since, her visit, as well as her services as a nurse, at an end. Roderick had long ago left the shelter of the verandah; he had taken his meals in the dining-room, or on the terrace, with Lorna and Martin. Nicholas came less frequently, and was preparing to go to sea; Florence and Woolly were in a state of uneasy seclusion; Stephanie was interviewing three tourist bureaus, which had written, unaccountably, to ask for her services, and spent most of her time on the road between Estronella and Gibraltar.

'Should have gone before,' said Roderick. 'But nothing's settled. That's why I've stayed on. Hope I haven't been too much in the way.'

'Not at all,' said Lorna politely.

He gave a sudden grin, and the years fell away suddenly and she saw him standing below her window on a summer's day, looking up at her and saying something. She could not remember what he had said, but she remembered, quite clearly, how he had looked. She found herself smiling back at that other Roderick, and then, at the look in his eyes, she stopped smiling and came back with a jerk to the present.

'Did you thank Carmela for nursing you so well?'

'I may have done. It was really your job, you know.'

'You said—'

'I know. So you were. Don't you ever feel you want to see England again?'

'Not often,' she said. 'Sometimes, when I don't feel very well, I get an odd feeling that I'd like to die and be buried there.'

'Can't understand how it is you don't get homesick. Don't you ever think of what spring's like?'

'There are so many springs,' said Lorna. 'There's the spring the poets talk about; there's the spring you see pictures of—a foam of blossom, beautifully photographed, or a carpet of daffodils in a park. The springs I remember were the ones that used to blow right through my thickest coats, through me, and out the other side. There was a faint promise of summer, with all the unpleasant remains of the damp winter cold. All the people who'd spent the winter abroad came back and told you they'd been sunbathing the day before yesterday. Everybody got flu and bronchitis, and had the chimneys swept too early. And Kate and Heloise used to drive all the maids mad by starting on what was known as the spring clean.'

'Well, all right. But you used to enjoy yourself in summer. You even played tennis, though it's impossible to look at you now, lounging about on terraces, and believe that you ever did anything active. You used to get up picnics and insist on my sitting out in the open and getting bitten by midges. And you used to enjoy—'

'I liked picking fruit and eating it off the trees, but I found that you couldn't do that in a garden run by Heloise. You had to wait until it came to table. Everything had to be just so; orderly; a procession of events year after year, with no change.'

'Nothing wrong with that.'

'I suppose not. I didn't find it exciting at the time, though. You shouldn't have shut me up in that house with your two sisters and gone away and left me.'

'My work was abroad; it was out in the open, too, in wild country, and you were expecting a baby. The first time, it was Nicholas; the next time, it was Martin. After that, it was too late. I wrote one short, hasty letter, and found myself without a wife.'

'If you'd loved me,' said Lorna, 'you would have come home. You would have—'

'I did come. But you didn't wait long, did you? If you'd really cared a hang for me, could you have thrown everything up so easily? I don't think so. If you'd stopped to think how much there was at stake, you wouldn't have taken that letter as final.'

'You didn't read it; you only wrote it.'

'I wrote it in a tent. I was trembling all over, I remember. Shaking like a ruddy aspen. I thought I had ague, but it wasn't ague. It was—'

'Rage.'

'A feeling of deadly frustration at being so far away from you. I wanted to be able to put my hands on you and—'

'Choke me.'

'Perhaps. I wouldn't have said I was a fellow with much imagination, but my God! it worked overtime then. I walked and walked and walked for hours, sweating it out and thinking of you in that fellow's arms.'

'He did once lift me up and carry me over

241

that bit of road that used to flood whenever the river rose. It was a long way from the house, but I daresay that Kate, with a pair of binoculars, could pick us out from the tower window.'

'You never spoke of yourself when you wrote to me. There was never any mention of yourself. Your letters were about the children, about my sisters, about the house. You never told me what you did, or what you thought, or how you felt without me.'

'I used to try, you know. But by that time, I'd realized that I was rather too unconventional for an English setting. Some of the things I put down used to strike me as being altogether too passionate. So I tore them up. I used to think that it was unfair, in any case, to write to a man all those thousands of miles away and get him into a state that I could do nothing to appease. I had much more imagination than you; I used to imagine you reading my letters and getting into a mood quite unsuitable for a man so far removed from his wife, and going in a frenzy out into the jungle to pick the first dusky belle you came across. I didn't see any point in that.'

'I didn't need letters. I only had to lie and think about you.'

'And how about the dusky belles?'

'I forget. It's a long time ago.'

'Yes. But we must have been in love, mustn't we,' mused Lorna.

'Too much so to throw it all away the first

242

time anything blew up. That was all your doing.'

She made no answer. They were in her sitting-room. She had not invited him into it; he had gone in search of her, knocked and entered. He was sitting in a deep chair, and she saw him looking round him with interest and more than a suspicion of disapproval.

'What's the matter?' she asked him lazily. 'Most people admire this room.'

'I don't say it isn't cool, and I suppose it's pretty. But I don't understand how you can let yourself sink back in all this luxury.'

'What should I do, then? I can't sell it and give the proceeds to the poor, because it isn't mine—except on paper. I've always regarded it as Salvador property. I've changed a good deal of it, and improved it, I hope, but I've never felt more than a rather privileged tenant.'

'Well, I don't like it,' said Roderick bluntly. 'There's a great deal too much of it.'

'Furniture? Surely not.'

'Luxury. Comfort's a great thing, up to a point, but it goes beyond that point at Casa del Carmen. This waiting on you, hand and foot. It's wrong. It's one of the things I've got against Carmela as a wife for Nicholas. What's a girl brought up like that going to do in England? Nobody in England's going to put her shoes on for her and run and fetch her handkerchief.'

'She—'

'Nobody's going to follow her round seeing she's got everything she wants. Nobody's going to stand at her elbow waiting for orders. What training is that for a hardy wife for a man?'

'Why does she have to be hardy? Nicholas isn't an Eskimo.'

'She'll have to do a day's work—ordering, planning, giving a hand here and there, even washing up now and again when the servants are out. That's if they can afford servants at all, and if they can get them if they can afford them. Can you imagine Carmela ironing Nicholas' shirts? Now, can you?'

'Aren't there laundries?'

'At a fantastic figure, yes, but as far as I can see they boil hell out of all the clothes they handle. If you want your shirts to last—and you do, at the price you have to pay for them—then you have to have them done carefully, at home. You've been out of England too long. Things aren't the same now as they used to be.'

'Well, don't get too morbid, Roderick. If Carmela's set up in a modern home with decent equipment, she'll manage. You've lived so long at Wychall that you've probably lost touch with all the later developments in labour-saving equipment. They've brought out all sorts of appliances that the modern housewife straps herself into before doing a whirlwind tour round the house.'

'I haven't lost touch with anything. You've
244

lost touch, living out here in this Nights-of-Gladness set-up, on a coast that attracts every kind of trash from all over the world. Villas and casas and palaces, all full of anybody but natives. All the self-styled artistic crowd, arriving with an easel or two and then propping up the local bar until it's time to move on. Riff-raff from every country, settling down for a spell, living on the cheap and then driving on to the next collection of fishing boats or the next huddle of houses painted boiled salmon. Long-haired boys in blue trousers and girls burnt nigger brown with their legs showing. If people have a country of their own, my own feeling is that they ought to have roots in it. There's nothing against seeing the world, or getting to know other countries, or having a look round—I've nothing against any of that kind of travel. What I object to is this selection of characters who walk up and down the fringes of the Mediterranean or the Caribbean like a lot of cats up and down an alley.'

'You make me see my friends in a new light,' said Lorna.

'You can smile, but living out here all the time, away from your own country, I think you have the worst of it. You can't make permanent friends, because the people you'd like as friends have decent homes and like to go back to them as often as possible.'

'Some people rather dislike the English
245

climate.'

'What's the matter with the climate? It doesn't get stinkingly hot in summer, and it doesn't get piercingly cold either. It's temperate, and it's for temperate people. Why don't you go back and settle down there, Lorna?'

'Because my home is out here.'

'Nonsense!'

'Perhaps I like having my shoes put on and my handkerchief fetched.'

'Then get where you've got to do your own fetching, and become a woman again.'

'Thank you; I think I'll stay here and be my own kind of woman.'

He began to speak, closed his mouth firmly and then, with deep thankfulness, saw the danger of the moment receding. He felt a dampness on his brow, and resisted an inclination to take out his handkerchief and mop it. His only safe course lay in silence. If he began to speak, if he began to tell her what kind of a woman he thought she was, if he told her why he wanted her to come home, the fight would be over before his forces had been assembled. He was not yet sure what he was going to fight for; all he knew was that desire had stirred in him, and was mounting warmly and steadily. If he spoke or acted too soon, he would frighten her or, worse, he would antagonize her still further. His only hope lay in maintaining his attitude of unshaken coolness and in coming upon her gently, secretly. He had come out here with no other thought but that of attempting to regain his influence over his two sons. If he had dreamed of this ... But he had come, and he had seen her, and no man in his senses—no man with his senses would be able to turn his back on this newly found beauty and grace and softness. But he had been close to wrecking his hopes; he had been about to give way to impulse, and if he gave way now she would throw him out of this pink-icing palace and never admit him again. He must be careful. He would be careful.

He roused himself to find she was on her feet. He rose, and with a last, unreadable glance round the room, followed her outside and along to the drawing-room.

'I heard Nicholas' car,' she said.

'Were you expecting him?'

'He said he might be able to come. He's bringing Captain Freeman with him; they're both lunching here.'

Nicholas was alone and in good spirits. Lorna, noting his air of well being, experienced a small pang. He was going—so soon—and he was leaving the girl he hoped to marry; he was also leaving his mother. He looked, under these melancholy circumstances, extremely cheerful. She reminded herself that he was young and that he would not be away long, that at his age cares sat lightly. At the end of it she found herself wishing he had looked a little—ever so little—sobered.

'Where's Marty?' he asked.

'He's in Florence's room.'

that he couldn't even telephone. I took him to the airport. Now I'll go and find Martin.'

He went to the door and opened it, but before he went out, his eyes rested for a moment—briefly, but with a keen scrutiny—on his father's face. A suspicion, formless as yet, welled up in Lorna, and she followed Nicholas' glance and turned to study Roderick's face. He looked at the two pairs of eyes and bore their scrutiny unflinchingly.

'Who's this you're talking about?' he enquired, with an air of a man whose mind, for the moment, has been elsewhere. A grin appeared on Nicholas' face and was instantly suppressed.

'One of Mama's boy-friends,' he said. 'Vanished.'

'Is that so?' said Roderick. 'Strange.'

'Very strange,' said Lorna slowly, her eyes on him. 'Very, very strange.'

'So there you have it,' said Nicholas, in conclusion. 'I would have told you before, Marty, but I had to think it out, and as a matter of fact, now I've—'

'I know,' said Martin. 'You wonder why the hell you d-didn't think of it before. It solves everything, in a way.'

'Not really. But you see why—'

'Yes. And I agree, it's the only possible

thing. I suppose I ought to say something like—'

'No. Say it later.'

'All right. But I'm glad, anyhow. You see, it makes it easier for me, too. I've been hanging about lately, hoping you'd do it this way, but it wasn't exactly a suggestion I felt I could make to you. There was too much responsibility attached to it. It wasn't my life, after all.'

'I've felt a different chap, these last few days.'

'I noticed something—and wondered. One thing I'd like to say is that I think you're a lucky chap.'

'Thanks; I know that, only too well. Have you made up your mind what you're going to do?'

'Yes. It isn't quite clear yet, but it's c-clearing. When I've got it straight, I'll let you know. Well ... good luck.'

'Thanks,' said Nicholas.

CHAPTER SEVENTEEN

'It's time I went,' said Roderick, for the second time.

He said it with rather more conviction, and Lorna looked at him questioningly. He had said nothing, for some days, about leaving. He had fallen into the ways of the household, and now appeared as permanent a member as Florence. The two avoided each other and Lorna found herself spending more and more time with Roderick on the sunny terrace, or sitting in a long chair on his verandah watching him as he walked to and fro with a limp that grew daily more pronounced. She admitted to herself, with some apprehension, that she had grown to like his company, and explained the fact by deciding that when he chose to put himself out to be pleasant, he could be an amusing companion. She watched for disquieting signs and saw none; he appeared to have called a truce. He was going up to Yago on the following day to see Don Manrique and his family, and although Lorna knew that he was to put before them his proposal that Nicholas and Carmela should wait a year before becoming engaged, the manner of the proposal seemed to have lost some of its arrogance, and now appeared more in the nature of a suggestion. He walked down to Woolly's house and brought him up to meals; he went for

'I couldn't have said he was a hairdresser, because he's in the hat trade.'

'Hat trade?'

'I told you,' said Woolly reproachfully. 'Charlie figured that if mantillas have gone out, hats have got to come in. So he's all set up in the hat trade in Spain, waiting.'

'Oh. Is he doing well?'

250

'No, he's not doing well, but he's waiting, because he says it's a good idea and they'll come round to buying his hats in time.'

'Oh. How long has he—'

'He's been here seventeen years, but he's doing a bit of trading on the side now, waiting till they get the hat habit.'

It sounded an uncertain future and not one likely to attract Martin, but the latter had been working out his own ideas and was now ready to submit them to his father. He saw him talking to Lorna out on the terrace, and made his way towards them.

'By the way, Lorna,' Roderick was saying, 'I wrote to Portalloway about something, and I had a letter from him. He's made me an offer for that mandarin screen you used to like. Handsome offer, too, but I don't know whether to let the screen go or not.'

'No, don't. At least, it's yours—you must do as you like.'

'You were fond of it once. If I thought you'd ever come over and look at it, I'd keep it.'

'I ... Here's Martin,' said Lorna, with deep relief. 'You can ask him. Martin, shall your father sell the mandarin screen for a handsome price?'

'No,' said Martin. 'You're looking very pretty, Mother.'

'That would sound even more charming, Martin,' she said, 'if you brought it out without that air of surprise.'

251

'Sorry, darling. But you always look so y-young, and that does rather surprise me. Arithmetic was my good subject.'

'Sit down and talk, darling.' Lorna leaned over and pulled a chair closer to her own, and Martin settled into it comfortably.

'That's what I came for,' he explained. 'To talk. I saw you both from afar and saw that both of you were alone, if you f-follow me, and so I came to talk about something.'

'About what?' asked Roderick, propping himself up against the balustrade and lighting a cigarette.

'About me,' said Martin.

'Go ahead,' said Roderick.

'It's about a job.' Martin addressed both his parents impartially. 'I've been thinking about it a lot, and I've decided what I want to do, and I've come to ask you if I can do it.'

'He always starts off like that, Lorna,' explained Roderick. 'He opens with diffidence, and gives you the idea that a word of dissent from you will blow his plans to pieces. Two hours later, you're still arguing and he hasn't moved an inch. Three hours later, he's—'

'He's stuck out his chin'—Martin smiled at his mother—'and turned into his papa all over again.'

'Well, let's have it,' said Roderick.

'I'd like to go to Canada with Woolly,' said Martin slowly.

There was a silence. It lasted a long time, and

252

Roderick was the first to break it.

'Those blasted flowers,' he said.

'No.' Martin took his mother's wrist and fingered her bracelet absently. 'No, not the flowers. But here's how I see it: I like Woolly. He—well, I l-like him. He's odd in a lot of ways, and if you didn't know how deep down his sense goes, you might be misled into thinking that he hadn't g-got any, but he has. I like the way his mind works, and I like—well, I like everything about him. I don't know the first thing about Canada, but they tell me it's a place you can get on in, if you work. And Woolly's job—his real job—is buying and selling horses. I don't know how to buy or sell them, but I know pretty well everything else about them. He says that—if I want it—he'll give me a job. He says it'll be a hard job, but at any rate it'll be out in the open and it'll be with horses, and that would suit me.'

'But, Martin—' began Lorna.

'Wait a minute, Mother. I know what you're going to say, and I'm coming to that. I never wanted to make the flowers a real business, as you know. I never saw it that way. But Woolly's got the idea that he'd like to go round to all these friends of his and talk to them about it, and so we've agreed that if he ever finds anybody out there who'll buy the idea, well—they can have it. I'll go on playing at it when I've bedded the horses down; it'll make a nice change. I don't suppose I could stop adding to

253

my collection even if I wanted to, it's a sort of h-habit, after all these years. But I wouldn't like to make it my business in life. I'd like to get into the horse business with Woolly and later, when he's past coming over to Europe and looking round for new stock, I can see to that side of it for him.'

He came to an end, and there was another silence. Martin looked from one of his parents to the other, and then put a mild query.

'Well?' he asked.

'You needn't ask me,' said Lorna, 'because your father was quite right when he said that I haven't any right to order your affairs.'

'I never in my life,' said Roderick, deeply incensed, 'said anything of the kind. You make a remark to a woman, and she twists it inside out and gives it back to you in a damned mangled form.'

'Well, I'd like to say that I like everything about the idea except the one fact: that you're proposing to go away just as I've got you back.'

'I know,' said Martin gently. 'But you're not exactly destitute, Mother darling. There are jet planes speeding across the Atlantic, taking l-lonely mothers to their s-sorrowing sons. There are nice comfortable ships. You and Father could come out every summer to visit me. That is ... if Father liked the idea of my going out there.'

'It sounds like sense to me,' said Roderick. 'It's the first time you've ever come to me with a

254

sound, straightforward—'

'You knew he loved horses,' said Lorna. 'Why couldn't you have thought of a job like this for him long ago?'

'My . . . God!,' said Roderick, when he could speak. 'You sit there and—and tell me that I haven't sweated my—my inside out for years, trying to place a blasted, pig-headed—'

'I could have told you that this would have been just the thing for him,' said Lorna. 'Ever since he was so high, he—'

'He's been nothing but a damned mule. He—'

'I know where he got that.'

'I've crawled on my hands and knees to people I thought would be able to help him. I've crawled on my hands and knees to anybody with influence in—' he told me that there were women in Europe working in fields, in the hot sun, and women working day and night in mills and factories, and women working themselves to the bone to keep body and soul together, and because of them I couldn't have any more money. Now he's completely off the subject again, and we shall get no further.'

'I shall go down and see this man Woolly, and I shall talk to him on sane and sound business lines; if he can convince me in the first place that he owns a sound business and can furnish reassuring figures, if he can prove to me that there's a good future in it for Martin, then

255

I shan't stand in the way. But I am not going to throw myself enthusiastically into a scheme of which I don't know the first thing. When I can get up to see Don Manrique, I shall talk to him along the same lines. He's a reasonable fellow, and he's got a good head; he'll see that I'm as anxious to do the best for my son as he is to do the best for his daughter. But I will not be harried into unwise decisions merely because my sons have got hold of a foolish fancy and want to indulge it.'

'Well, nobody harried you,' said Lorna. 'There was no need to lose your temper.'

'I did not lose my temper. Martin will tell you that I'm not disposed, as a rule, to let myself go. I can behave as reasonably as any other man, but you always knew exactly how to work me into a state. We hadn't been married ten minutes before you were practising the gentle art of bull-baiting. I never thought of it before, but it must have been your Spanish instincts.'

'You always put everything down to my Spanish blood, always. All the things you didn't like.'

'And I was right. A cool, sensible Englishwoman would never have rushed out as you did and left two helpless children and a man who would have given his life for her. Just at the drop of a hat. It was two long, miserable years before I could get myself to go into your room again.'

'Would you rather I w-went and—'

'No. Stay where you are, Martin,' said Lorna. 'He's only trying to hurt me.'

'There'd only be justice in it, if I did. You gave me years of long, lonely hell.'

'You weren't the only one. Try marrying somebody you don't love and who's in love with someone else, and then see. Try living without children, separated from your babies and cut adrift from someone you thought you could depend on.'

'I was prepared to go across the world to find you and bring you back, but not from another man's arms. I could have—stay where you are, Martin. We're here, after all, to discuss your affairs.'

'Well, discuss them without me,' said Lorna.

'You know very well we can't do that. You're their mother and you owe them something for depriving them of a mother's care at the age at which they most needed it. You owe me something, too, though I won't drag myself in. You owe me nearly twenty lonely years.'

'Juan Salvador died eight years ago. You couldn't have been very lonely then, or you would have written a line of some kind of sympathy.'

'I didn't know the first thing about it until I heard—quite by chance—that you'd left Madrid and gone to stay in the Salvador home somewhere in the south. That was enough for

257

me. If you wanted to stay where he belonged, you could stay there and there was no point in trying to drag your mind back to matters you'd probably long forgotten. And you were right to come here. It suits you. It's a beautiful frame for a beautiful picture, and you look part of it—elegant, lovely, and completely removed from the dust of ordinary existence. This is where you belong, lifted up, high up above rough contacts and rough men and their rough advances. You made that pretty plain when I first got here. You looked like a toothy morsel placed high out of a small boy's reach: he could see, he could even smell—but he couldn't touch. And so you can—My God! Lorna, Lorna, Lorna, my darling, don't cry! Don't cry, my darling. Lorna, I'll do anything. I'll cut my tongue out, I swear it, and I'll ... Lorna, please! Darling Lorna, don't cry! Please, please. Look, I'm here. I'm kneeling here beside you, as I've been kneeling ever since you went away; I've been praying for your return, but you never came back. I'm a rough brute, darling ... will you—Martin, give me your handkerchief ... he's not there. Look, here's mine ... blow. That's better. Will you look at me, just once, kindly, and I swear I'll never ... Lorna, I love you, and I'm sorry. Put your head there, my sweet ... quiet now. I'm a sour devil, and I love you. I've always loved you. Are you comfortable? There, that's better. Don't say anything. You're so lovely, so lovely. You're—

Now look, you Natalio or whatever they call you, you just go away, d'you hear? Nobody called you. That's the idea, go on. Lorna, you're hysterical. Pull yourself together and—'

'That wasn't Natalio, R-Roderick. It was C-Carlos.'

'Well, I didn't call him, either. Too many of them hanging round. Lorna—'

Here it was. It was coming.

'Well?'

'Look, Lorna, this situation is really rather ridiculous, you know. You'd much better marry me and be done with it.'

CHAPTER EIGHTEEN

'We are happy, no?' said Carmela.

'Lie still,' said Nicholas. 'I never knew a girl for turning in a diagnosis at the oddest times. We are suited, no? We are thirsty, no? We are together, no?'

'Kiss me, please.'

'There. All right?'

'No.'

'There. Better?'

'Yes, thank you. Nicholas—'

'Well?'

'I am so glad that we are here.'

He made no reply; there was no need for a reply. They were here; she was lying in his arms and her body—warm and petal soft—was against his. He could see, through the window of their room, the outline of the hills, and he could hear round their little mountain retreat the sounds which had become familiar to him throughout his courtship, and which blended with the murmur of Carmela's voice and the thudding of his heart. They had met one another, fallen in love with one another in the shelter of the hills, and it was fitting that they should lie now in their protective shadows.

'I love you very much,' murmured Carmela, against his cheek.

He kissed her gently, almost absently. He was thinking of their future and measuring it in terms of his own big, hard body and the tiny, untried one which lay in his embrace. She was to be the mother of his children—this dainty, delicately fashioned child. She was to bear them and nourish them; she had left the soft little nest in which she had been so carefully tended and she was to follow him wherever the dictates of his profession chanced to send him. Her body was in his arms, and her trustful spirit and their joint, unknown future was in his care.

A weight came from nowhere and settled on him and he identified it, incredulously, as a sense of responsibility. He tested it carefully and felt his strength rising to meet its challenge. His grasp of his beloved tightened protectively.

'You love me, no?' said Carmela.

'No. I'm just hanging on to you to see you don't fall off.'

'Why should I fall off?'

'Because I feel twice the man I was. I'm growing careworn.'

'I shall look after you.'

'Thank you. Carmela, have you any idea of the kind of house you'd like to live in?'

'Yes. A house like that one you showed me in that picture.'

'You mean the riverside cottage?'

'Yes.'

'That's no good in winter; every time the Thames rises, the drawing-room carpet gets up and swims.'

'Can we keep a goat? My mother says that goats' milk is best for children.'

'I don't think we'd be popular if we kept one in town, but if we've got a bit of land somewhere, I'll buy you one.'

'Will you learn Spanish?'

'If you like. Though it seems to me I've come a pretty long way without any.'

'Will you be sorry, ever, that you did not marry an English girl?'

'If I am, what shall I do? Throw you back and ask for a change?'

'No. I am yours for ever and ever and ever. Nicholas—'

'Darling?'

'Will they be angry?'

'No, I don't think so. Why should they be?

We've saved them a lot of trouble, and a lot of expense, too. And a hell of a lot of argument.'

'Your mother will be glad.'

'Yes, and yours. It's our respective papas who'll paw the ground angrily.'

'We shall not think about them now. You have only two more days with me, and then ...'

'You'll write every day, won't you, Carmela? Just write down whatever comes, and fold it up at the end of each day and address it and post it. Promise!'

'I promise. Darling, darling Nicholas.'

'I wonder if your father's there by now.'

Don Manrique was there, facing Roderick on the verandah.

'Well, all right,' said Roderick. 'Tell me.'

'They were married yesterday,' said Don Manrique. 'When I got the news, I came down here at once.'

Roderick sat for some time in silence.

'I'm sorry,' he said at last.

'That they were married?'

'Yes and no. I'm sorry they did it this way.'

'Nicholas had a reason,' said Don Manrique.

'Obviously. Most young men in love can find reasons.'

'But he acted deliberately. Martin told me.'

'Martin knew of this.'

'Yes. Nicholas told him what he was going to do. He also told him when to look for me; he knew that when I got the news, I would come to you. He told Martin to watch for me.'

'Well?'

'Martin did more than to watch; he came up to meet me on the hill. He said that Nicholas had decided to marry at once, and in this way, because he thought that so he would take away the most important thing that is separating you from Lorna. Nicholas said to Martin that if there was a long delay, she and you would quarrel, and he did not want you to quarrel. He wants—'

'I see,' said Roderick. 'Well, it's done.'

'Yes, it is done. Perhaps it will be well.'

'I'll do all I can to see that it is. I suppose I needn't tell you that.'

'No. Thank you.'

'Are we to see Nicholas before he leaves?'

'Yes. He would like you, too, to take Carmela to see off his ship, and then she will come home to us when she returns.'

'I see,' said Roderick again.

He was feeling sorry for the man before him. Don Manrique had lost a daughter, his only child. Her future would be far away from the house up in the mountains. She would return, briefly, from time to time, but her absences would be long and she would be, for the most part, out of his reach.

'I'm sorry,' he said again, inadequately.

He walked out to the porch and stood watching Don Manrique mount.

'You will tell Lorna all that I have told you?'

263

asked Don Manrique, looking down.

'Nearly all.'

'Then, good-bye.'

'Half a moment,' said Roderick. He went back to his room and returned with a small piece of paper. 'Here,' he said, 'I've scribbled my name and address on that. Will you promise me something?'

'No,' said Don Manrique, with his slow smile.

'Listen to me carefully,' said Roderick. 'I'm a man who keeps his mouth shut.'

'So?'

'There's a good deal of the country round here that I haven't had a chance to see.'

'It is very interesting country.'

'That's what I think. If you've ever got time to show me round some of it, I'd be glad to go with you.'

'The mountains look different at night.'

'Will you send me word?'

'You and I are getting too old for games.'

'Some games. Come on Manrique, come on.'

'Very well, then,' said Don Manrique. 'I will send word.'

'Good man.'

'Adios.'

'Not Adios,' corrected Roderick. 'That's too final. What's that other one?'

'Hasta la vista,' said Don Manrique, and rode away.

'I don't want to know anything,' said Florence. 'I'm just saying that whether you do or whether you don't, I've got to move on.'

'I don't see why,' said Lorna.

'Because it's been wonderful, you've been wonderful, but it'll never be the same again. If you marry him, you'll go away; if you don't marry him, you'll marry somebody else.'

'I really don't see why,' said Lorna again.

'Well, you will,' prophesied Florence gloomily. 'It's a thing I've watched over and over again in women of your age. They live lives of comparative seclusion for years; men here and there, of course, especially when they're as beautiful as you are. It's a game; some women play it for fun and some play it seriously and some play it for stakes, but it's still a game. And then when they get round about your age, they fall in love, or they start wondering whether they ought to fall in love. Didn't it happen to me? I knew Leo van Leyte for six years without being too sure whether he was ever in the party or not, and then when I rounded my forties, I woke up one morning feeling terrible. When I'd diagnosed my symptoms, I went right out and hunted up Leo and I didn't rest till we were married.'

'But Florence, I've told you. I don't feel at all—'

'Lorna, that's neither here nor there. I don't know why a woman can't live out her life in peace, but that's the way it is. Just as she thinks she's reached a nice, quiet backwater, the current catches her and she's going round and round in circles again. This Roderick Saracen has started something; he probably doesn't know it, but I do. I can see the difference in you every day. You're not the same woman.'

'Well, I feel the same.'

'You don't look the same. You've lost that beautiful calm you used to have. You used to sit for hours, just gazing; you looked relaxed and at ease and at peace, and there wasn't a man in your mind—seriously, that is. Now you're not relaxed any more; you're withdrawn and detached and every now and then you smile to yourself. You used to be such a good listener, and now you float away in spirit and take your ears with you and I'm left to talk to myself, as I'm doing now. You're not even listening. If I went on talking in the same tone and told you that my grandmother died in a fit this morning, which she didn't, you wouldn't even hear me. Would you? I said would you. WOULD YOU?'

'Would I what?' asked Lorna.

'Nothing. I was just doing one of my little monologues.'

'I'm sorry, Florence. I was just—'

'You were just proving something, and proving it pretty conclusively. Well, I suppose I ought to wish you joy, but how can I? I can't stand the fellow.'

'Florence, you mustn't rush to conclusions.'

'Will you let me come and stay with you sometimes—wherever you are?'

'Don't be silly. Of course I will. But I shall be here.'

'No, you won't. And it won't occur to him—not once—that he's asking you to leave a kind of paradise. You know, Lorna, I thought of going back to Canada with Woolly and Martin. I might, but I don't think so. If I could get somebody to sell me a hunk of land hereabouts, I'd build me a nice little house, something like this one, only along baby lines. I've got to like looking out at oranges hanging off trees, and bunches of grapes growing in the sun, and little donkeys and men with straw hats. It's like me—slow and lazy and go-as-you-please. What are you laughing at?'

'You. You make yourself sound like someone in old clothes and a pair of rope-soled sandals, drinking in the Mediterranean atmosphere. There's nothing slow and lazy and go-as-you-please about you. You merely rest here between shopping sprees, that's all.'

'Well, don't begrudge them to me. I started out in check gingham and scratchy wool, and I washed for the family before I was eleven. What I've got now, I enjoy. But I've enjoyed life at the Casa del Carmen most of all, and I'm grateful to you.'

'Don't make it sound so final!'

'What's the difference?' said Florence, bleakly. 'It's over.'

267

'That's why I let things drift for so long,' said Martin, in the privacy of his father's room. 'I had to think a bit; it wasn't until Nicholas told me that he'd made up his mind that I went and asked Woolly about the job. Do you think Don Manrique was upset?'

'He's got something to be upset about. Nicholas has—'

'Well, somebody would have married Carmela eventually, I suppose.'

'Somebody in Spain, within reasonable visiting distance.'

'I wanted to tell you the news about N-Nick, but he said I was to leave it to Don Manrique. I'd rather have told you myself.'

'I understand,' said Roderick.

'About telling Mother ...'

'I'll do that.'

'Didn't she see Don Manrique?'

'No. He came round this way and I saw him here. He's a good fellow.'

'Yes. Father, there's just one t-thing I'd like to say.'

'Go ahead.'

'It's just that Nick and I ... he says to tell you he's on your side. I am, too.'

'Have I got a side?'

'We didn't know how Mother felt about ... everything. Nick and I thought that you might have some t-trouble getting her to know her own mind.'

'Women haven't got much in the way of

minds. Your mother's a beautiful woman, but she always had more harebrain than horse-sense. Most women have. Perhaps they don't need more.'

'Marrying you would be the most s-sensible thing to do.'

'That's the reason I'm afraid she won't do it.'

'Has she . . . refused?'

'She hasn't been asked yet—formally.'

'Oh.' Martin grinned. 'Well, anyway, as I said, Nick and I are with you. He says that if you can't bring it off alone, we'll come in with a bit of m-moral blackmail, threaten to withdraw our f-filial affection, as it were. We've got a bit of pull, you know.'

'I know.'

'It'll be nice to be a united family again.'

'Nicholas has gone; you're going. Not much unity about that.'

'Those are only the normal h-hazards, though. Children marrying, or going away. But if you and Mother get together, Nick and I will feel there's a home.'

'You're not the only ones,' commented Roderick.

'We'll be awfully h-happy if you bring it off.'

'You're not the only ones,' said Roderick again.

CHAPTER NINETEEN

The Panther was scarcely discernible, a mere smudge on the horizon, and fast disappearing. Lorna leaned against the window of the drawing-room, long after there was nothing to see, and stared out silently, thinking of Carmela and her parents, and Nicholas, and the look in his eyes as he kissed her and drove away from the house.

She had not gone to see him off. Roderick and Martin had gone, taking Carmela with them, and they were to bring her back to the Casa del Carmen. Behind Lorna, stiff and upright on the drawing-room sofa, sat Carmela's mother, waiting for their return, fanning herself, and no more disposed to conversation than Lorna herself was.

Martin drove Nicholas' little car back to the house. Behind him, with less speed but more state, came Roderick and his new daughter-in-law, who had waved Nicholas off with smiles, and who now, without warning, turned to Roderick and, clutching his sleeve convulsively, wept copiously into it. He felt unequal to doing more than patting her head now and then and saying, 'There, there now,' but he was sorry, on the whole, when she pushed her damp curls off her brow and wiped her eyes and ceased to cling to him. Stealing glances at her whenever he thought he could do so unobserved, he took in, for the first time, details of her face and figure, assessing them in the light of their durability. You never knew, he mused, with these foreign girls. They bloomed early and then, at an age at which the average Englishwoman was nearing her prime, they looked either overblown or dessicated. This little thing seemed to have good lines; she also had good bones and a skin that looked more delicate than most of these Southern European women. Soft, of course; not a well-developed muscle anywhere, but if they could get her over to England and induce her to walk a couple of miles a day, just as a beginning, they might build up some stamina. She had a good deal of dignity and more style than most girls of her age. She was, on the whole, more promising than he had ventured to hope, or that Nicholas had any right to expect.

Carmela, raising her eyes, encountered the grey ones on her with a look so unexpectedly benign that she retreated against the sleeve again; Roderick felt the moisture going through to his shirt sleeve.

'There, there,' he said, with a pat that Carmela recognized as fatherly. 'There now. He'll soon be back.'

He was pleasantly surprised when they reached the Casa del Carmen and he was presented to her mother; his newly awakened hopes rose still further as he noted that here was evidence of good wear, very good wear indeed. If Nicholas' wife wore as well as this—and there was no reason why she shouldn't, with a little good advice, and a little overlooking—then there would be nothing much to worry about.

Mother and daughter drove away, and Roderick stood on the steps of the porch watching them go, and looking so self-possessed, so much at home that Florence, returning from a visit to friends in the district, found herself fighting a strong inclination to go up to him and ask him if he thought he owned the joint. Instead, she achieved what she felt to be a distant courtesy.

'Nicholas get off all right?' she asked.

'Thank you, yes,' said Roderick.

'How was Carmela?'

'Very well, thank you. Very well, indeed.'

'I passed them just now. She looked rather pale.'

'No doubt she's a little tired.'

'I suppose so. Where's Lorna?'

'Lorna's in the drawing-room, I believe.'

This was as much as they usually got through without giving way to their mutual desire to part. Florence, however, was looking at him with a glance in which he saw an equal mixture of dislike and speculation.

'I shall be leaving tomorrow,' she said.

'So Lorna told me. I hope you have a good journey,' said Roderick politely.

'If you think you're driving me away,' said Florence stoutly, 'you're taking too much credit. I'm going because I think it's best for Lorna.'

There was no reply; the silence indicated sufficiently clearly that Roderick thought it best, too.

'I figure,' went on Florence hardily, 'that she's restless. I think the best thing for her would be to settle down and marry, in that order. She's got plenty of choice; all she has to do is to make up her mind.'

'No doubt,' said Roderick.

'She and Captain Freeman seemed to—'

'He has, unfortunately, left.'

'I know that. But Bill Charton—'

'Has also unfortunately gone away.'

'Gone?'

'Very suddenly. Very suddenly, indeed. His yacht was, so to speak, called away.'

'I suppose,' said Florence, throwing aside the hampering cloak of dignity, 'I suppose you think you're very clever.'

There was no reply; the cool grey eyes rested on her hopefully, awaiting further demonstrations. Florence made an effort, swallowed her anger and disappointment and spoke almost forlornly.

'I love Lorna,' she said. 'I think she's the nicest woman I ever met. I liked living here; I didn't cadge anything; I tried, in not too obvious ways, to pay my dues. I don't know

273

what you've got in mind for her, but the life we've led here for the past few months has been, in my opinion, as pleasant as any that you or anybody else could offer her. If you've got any affection at all for her, then just you think about it—if you can bring yourself to it—from her point of view, and not from yours. You want her, and if I know you, you want her on your own terms. Well, I hope, first, that she won't marry you; I hope, second, that if she does she'll do it with her eyes open, and I hope, third, that she won't live to regret it. That's all. Do you want to say anything?'

'Nothing at all, thank you,' said Roderick.

'I thought you wouldn't. Well, this is good-bye. We shan't meet again.'

'Good-bye,' said Roderick. 'I understand that it was you who asked your brother to come here.'

'Don't you say one word against Woolly. He's worth six of—'

'I am just going down to see him and to talk over with him the details of Martin's future.'

'You mean you're actually going to let Martin have a future?'

'If you care to phrase it like that, yes.'

'Then there's hope for you. Perhaps I was wrong about you, though I don't think so. Anyway, I apologize.'

'Not at all. Let me thank you for your help in the matter.'

'Not you; let Martin thank me, if he wants

to. I don't know how a man like you came to have a wife like Lorna, but people don't get what they deserve in this world.'

'I suppose not.'

'Well, good-bye.'

There was a perceptible pause, and an obvious struggle. Then Florence held out a hand and Roderick took it.

'Good-bye.'

'Good-bye.'

She was gone, not without dignity, and he turned and walked down to Woolly's waggon and saw that it was now, once more, a single unit, self-contained and ready for the road. Martin's truck had been brought down and stood beside it. The caravan was assembled and would soon be on the move.

Roderick stood looking at the two vehicles, and Woolly came out and stood beside him.

'How d'you get that outfit across the Atlantic?' enquired Roderick.

'That?' said Woolly, in surprise. 'My gosh, I don't. I've got a kind of small warehouse at Cherbourg that I rent. It all goes into that and it gets looked after until I come across and need it again. I don't take it with me, by gosh!'

'I came down to talk to you about Martin,' said Roderick. 'Are you busy?'

'Wait. I'll bring out chairs,' said Woolly.

They sat and talked peaceably, and Martin joined them. Dusk came, and then the stars appeared, but they still sat on, at ease.

'Don't mind telling you,' said Woolly, 'that you had me scared, once.'

'He scares everyone,' said Martin. 'But the bigger the d-dog, the gentler, don't they say?'

'Then they say wrong,' said Woolly. 'What became of that girl?'

'Which girl?' asked Martin.

'The girl who talked.'

'Oh, Stephanie? She went.'

'I'm glad. Where'd she go?' enquired Woolly.

'She's in a job that suits her,' said Roderick. 'She's rounding tourists up into obedient little groups, and marching them round and lecturing to them.'

They sat silent, sympathizing with the tourists. Time went on and they still stayed there, silent or talking, smoking, at peace.

'Grand night,' said Woolly, at last.

'You both ought to turn in early, if you're starting at dawn,' advised Roderick, rising to his feet. 'I'll get back to the house.'

'I'll go with you,' said Martin.

There was a pause, and then Roderick's voice came calmly through the darkness.

'No, you won't,' he said.

In the darkness, Martin Saracen smiled.

Roderick walked slowly. The lights of the house shone in front of him; as he approached them, he felt for the first time a sinking of the spirit. Something struggling up through his confidence in the eventual triumph of common sense whispered that women were unpredictable creatures and not given to reasoning. He knew what was best for Lorna, and he was going in now to tell her so, but it was just possible that after these years of living alone and doing everything she chose, regardless of its fitness, she had grown resentful of advice, however sound. But it was no use standing out here, speculating. The thing to do was to go in and have it out, once and for all ... for it would be once and for all. If she wanted him, she could have him—now. He wasn't going to travel to and fro between his home and hers, doing the journey on his knees. He was a man and she was a woman. She was beautiful, but he was a whole man; a man who had kept himself in good trim, who had kept rules and skirted most temptations. He could only offer himself as he was. Anybody who didn't think he was good enough could go further and, he might tell himself without undue conceit, fare a good deal worse. If remembering a woman—off and on—for nearly twenty years, if keeping her image in his heart and avoiding most other women for her sake—if that wasn't enough, then it ought to be. Her room at home was as she had left it. If that wasn't in the best tradition of mourning-without-ceasing, then he'd like someone to tell him what was, that was all.

Well, he could only ask her and get it over with. He'd go in there and find her.

It took some time to find her. She had left the drawing-room, and she was neither in her rooms nor in his. Even the servants, to whom, conquering his unwillingness, he at last appealed in irritated gestures, did not know where she was to be found.

He ran her down, at last, in Martin's room. She was standing before his suit-cases, counting small heaps of underclothing.

'Oh, hello, Roderick,' she said.

He could not help feeling that it was a bad setting, and that she had chosen it deliberately. No man could speak his piece while a woman counted underpants. He frowned, hesitated, and then sat on the end of his son's bed.

'Why can't Martin do this himself?' he asked sourly. 'Or one of those servants?'

Lorna looked at him abstractedly.

'You know, Roderick, I don't know what he *does* with his clothes,' she said. 'When he came here, I bought him an entire stock. He looked—for a week—almost respectable. And then it all began to fall to pieces. His beautiful flannels are nothing but horse's hairs, and there's paint all over his good shirts, and his jackets are all torn. What does he *do* to everything?'

'What does it matter what he does to everything? He's going to Canada where they wear check shirts and dungarees.'

'He's going to England first, and he's going across the Atlantic in a perfectly respectable

Canadian-Pacific cabin. He can't wear dungarees on board.'

'Well frankly, I don't care. I want to talk to you.'

'Talk away,' invited Lorna calmly. 'Wait a minute ... three, four—that's only four of them. I bought him six.'

It could only be deliberate. No woman—not even this woman, who appeared to have an obstinate streak—could behave like this when she knew perfectly well what a man was after. She was doing it to put him off, that was it. This was her way of evading the issue, but if she thought that he was a man who was going to perch on the end of a bed while she pretended to pack suit-cases, she was damn well underestimating him.

'Will you stop doing that and listen to me?'

'There's no need to be violent, Roderick.'

'I'm not being violent.'

'Yes, you are. Martin's leaving at dawn. Anything you want to say can surely wait until after he's gone, can't it?'

'No, it can't. You've had a long string of excuses for the past few days to keep me at arm's length, and I'm tired of it. If you want to get rid of me, you know the way to do it. You don't have to hide in a bedroom counting socks. You can be honest and open.'

'Very well, then. Please go away until I've packed Martin's things.'

'Martin doesn't want his things packed.

Martin's been brought up to pack his own things. Packing other people's things when they're not there to see you do it is crass stupidity, anyway; all he'll do when he comes in is turn the whole lot out again to see what's inside. You're wasting your time.'

'Then perhaps you'll—'

'And your wasting mine.'

'That's too bad,' said Lorna.

'For God's sake, Lorna, will you please—'

'Will you please stop shouting?'

'I am not shouting.'

'You are shouting. You always do shout. You're like a person talking to foreigners and shouting because he thinks they'll understand better if he yells. You think that shouting will make people understand what you want, and you think that if you shout even more loudly, they'll agree to anything you want them to do. Well, some of them may, but I was never frightened of you, whether you shouted or whether you didn't.'

'Have you finished?'

'Yes. You can go away now.'

'I have no intention of going away until you've listened to what I've got to say.'

'I know what you've come to say. You've been saying it without stopping ever since you set foot in this house. You've said it by frightening all my friends away and when they've refused to be frightened away, you've had them sent away. You terrified poor Woolly

280

and you tried to cow Florence, and you used your influence in the beastliest way to get Oliver Freeman sent away, and you said something to Bill Charton to make him feel he ought to take himself off. You tried to frighten poor little Carmela, and you would have gone up to Yago and shouted at Don Manrique if you hadn't happened to join him in that incredibly juvenile escapade. You couldn't frighten Nicholas and Martin, because they inherited, thank God, enough of your hardness to protect them. And now you're trying to frighten me. You're—'

'Lorna, I swear to you that—'

'—trying to browbeat me into leaving this beautiful house, in which I've been so happy, and marry you and leave this lovely place and this lovely climate and bury myself in that great gloomy grey mansion all your ancestors were born in, just because you think it's a tidier way of keeping the family together than to have you there and me here and the boys everywhere. Your sole aim is to—'

'Lorna, I love you. I—'

"—is to bring this about, regardless of what I feel about it, or what—'

'Lorna, I came to—'

'—or what's best for me, or—'

'—ask you—'

'—whether I've got any feelings—'

'—to—'

'—in the matter at all. You pretend to love

281

me, and all you think of is yourself and your—'

'—marry me.'

'—own feelings. My dear Roderick, let me tell you quite clearly that the only reason I'm marrying you is because—'

'Good God!'

'—is because Nicholas wants Carmela to go and live in England, and I am not going to have that poor little child going through this same dreadful experience—'

'What in the devil's name was dreadful about—'

'—without someone to be kind to her, and to protect her, and to help her over the early difficulties. She's not going to be torn from her home and left to struggle along in that great house without any love or—'

'Good God, I worshipped you!'

'—or kindness or gentleness, or—'

'Kate and Heloise were the kindest pair of women that ever—'

'—or help. She's going to have a mother, myself, and when Nicholas' children are born, I'm going to be there to watch over them and—'

'Can I—'

'—and love them and—'

'—be there too?'

'—and to . . . what did you say?'

'I said can I be there too?'

'Be where?'

'You're in my home, being a kind mother

and a gentle grandmother. I merely asked if I could be there too. I wasn't a bad father, on the whole, and I don't suppose I'll make a bad grandfather, when it comes to it. I—Put those clothes down, Lorna.'

'I'm going to—'

'Put them DOWN.'

'You needn't start—'

'If you pick up one more shirt or sock or handkerchief, I shall forget myself and I shall hit you.'

'You'll *what?*'

'Hard.'

'Do you call yourself a man?'

'I do. If you'll come over here, I'll show you on what grounds I—Very well, then, I'll come over there.'

'Tomorrow,' said Lorna.

'Now. Come here and ... now take back all those lies.'

'No, Roderick.'

'You're coming home for one reason and one reason only. You know it and I know it. The boys know it. Your friend Florence knows it. I've told you I love you, and I've crawled on my knees begging you to marry me ... instead of bringing you to your senses like this. Lorna, you're very sweet ... but you didn't tell the truth. Did you? Did you? Will you say it, or shall I shake it out of you?'

'I love you,' said Lorna.